LOVING JESSIE'S GIRL

Love on the Double Series - Book 1

L.A. REMENICKY

Lavish Publishing LLC

First Edition

Love on the Double Series, Book 1

2016 Lavish Publishing, LLC

All Rights Reserved

Published in the United States by Lavish Publishing, LLC, Midland, Texas

Paperback Edition

Cover Design by: Wyked Ink

Cover Images: Adobe Stock

ISBN: 9781944985141

www.LavishPublishing.com

Contents

Chapter One

THE GROUND RUSHED past faster and faster as the wheels of the airplane lost their contact with the runway. AJ unconsciously rubbed his right leg, lost in thought. He had been teaching his fifth period creative writing class when the pain first hit, sudden and white-hot, causing him to stop in the middle of a sentence.

"You okay, Mr. Monroe?" one of his students asked.

"Yeah." He leaned against the desk, taking the weight off of his leg. "Now, let's get back to work."

The bell rang ten minutes later, signaling the end of the class. His students gathered their books, talking back and forth.

"Don't forget your short stories are due next week," he said loud enough to be heard over the sounds of shuffling as he grabbed his phone out of his desk drawer and selected Jessie's cell number. His call immediately went to voicemail. "Hey, Jess. Call me when you get this. What's going on with your leg? Just call me, Bro."

"Sir? Would you like something to drink?" the stewardess asked, bringing him back to the present.

"I'll take a water, please," he replied, trying to forget the feeling of dread he experienced when he couldn't reach Jessie earlier. He smiled at the stewardess when she handed him a bottle of water and a glass of ice with a bag of pretzels. He pulled his phone out of his pocket and plugged in his ear buds, wanting the music to distract him from his thoughts. The throbbing in his leg was still there bringing back the worry. The last time he felt pain like this was two years ago when Jessie was shot while serving as a marine in Afghanistan. The first time was when they were twelve and Jessie fell out of a tree and broke his wrist.

After almost missing his connecting flight at O'Hare in Chicago, AJ was exhausted and grateful when he found a taxi willing to drive him to Woodview, about twenty miles outside Fort Wayne, without charging him an outrageous fee.

The sun dropped below the horizon as the taxi pulled up in front of Jessie's house. The windows were dark, and his work truck was not in the driveway. AJ tried calling Jessie's cell again before he got out of the cab. Still no answer. He paid the driver, slipping him a twenty dollar tip, and walked up the steps to the porch. He banged on the door loudly enough for Jessie to hear it if he were home.

"Looks like no one is home. Do you need a ride to a motel?" the taxi driver asked, still idling in the driveway.

"No need. I know where he keeps the spare key," AJ

replied as he walked around the house to the back yard. He grinned when he saw the plastic owl sitting on the corner post of the deck. He lifted the owl and found the spare key taped to the bottom just where he knew it would be. He unlocked the door and walked into the house, keeping his eyes open for any clues as to Jessie's whereabouts. Nothing was out of place, and there was no sign of Jessie. After waving to the cab driver, he shut and locked the front door.

AJ checked the fridge and found nothing but a couple cans of beer. Jessie loved to cook, so he had clearly planned to be gone. He took his bag into the spare bedroom and decided to start looking for Jessie first thing in the morning; stumbling around town in the dark wouldn't accomplish anything. After taking a shower, AJ pulled out his laptop and his glasses to work on his manuscript, hoping it would take his mind off his missing brother and the throbbing pain in his leg.

The sun blazed in through the picture window and woke him from his dreams. His stomach rumbled as he searched his bag for the power cord to his laptop; falling asleep with it on had drained the battery.

After a shower and an unsuccessful search for coffee, he took the keys to Jessie's vintage truck from their place on the hook near the door. First stop was breakfast and coffee before he could start his search for his missing brother.

When he turned the key, the roar of the engine brought the memories of the two of them restoring the vehicle to the surface. They rebuilt the engine and spent countless hours sanding and welding until the truck body looked just the way they wanted it. His 1972 'Cuda was supposed to have been their next project, but their falling out over a girl had prompted Jessie to join the Marines instead. It took his brother almost losing his leg in Afghanistan for them to start talking again.

Shaking his head to disperse the memories, he pushed the stick shift into first gear and drove away from the garage toward town.

Chapter Two

RINA ABBOTT CLUTCHED the mug of coffee tighter as another shiver wracked her body. Knowing Jessie had planned to be away until Tuesday, she was surprised to see him drive past without a wave or his customary toot of the truck's horn.

She pulled herself up and stepped off the porch. "C'mon, Petey," she called to her Jack Russell Terrier. She walked across the yard toward the path, which wound along the stream, leading to Jessie's front yard. He would probably be back before she could walk the distance to his house.

Her vision wavered in and out as she stumbled down the path, her determination to reach her best friend the only thing keeping her moving forward. Once she reached his front porch, she lost consciousness and crumpled down on the steps.

With a bag of groceries in one hand and a steaming cup of coffee in the other, AJ ambled up the front walk, dropping both when he noticed the beautiful woman sprawled out on the porch steps.

"Hey, are you okay?" he asked as he reached toward her, stopping when the dog on the porch growled at him. "It's okay, boy. I just want to help." He held the back of his hand out to the animal, scratching its ears when it sat and looked at him expectantly.

He touched her arm, alarmed at the heat radiating off her. Brushing her blonde hair away from her face, he was distracted by the curve of her cheek, his fingers itching to trace it, before he noticed the pallor of her skin and bright spots of red on her cheeks. Her clothes were baggy as if she lost weight and hadn't bought new clothes that fit.

She shifted and opened her eyes. "Love you, Jessie," she mumbled. He looked into her eyes, mesmerized by the hazel color until she passed out again.

"Jessie lucked out this time. You're gorgeous," he murmured as he dialed 911 on his cell phone.

Frustrated as he answered "I don't know" to most of the dispatcher's questions, he wondered how long it would take for an ambulance to get there. He rubbed his neck as he listened for the wail of a siren. Anger welled up as he wondered how his brother could leave his girl-friend here alone when she was obviously sick.

The siren cut off as the ambulance screeched to a halt. Pushing a gurney, the EMTs hurried over to the porch, dropping down to check over Rina. The younger EMT looked up at AJ. "Hey, Jessie. I thought you weren't going to be back until Tuesday. Why didn't you let the dispatcher know it was you?"

"I'm not Jessie." He wasn't even in town for a full day, and people already thought he was his brother.

"Shit. You must be AJ. I'm Cam." He began to question AJ about finding Rina.

"So what happened here?" Cam asked, removing the stethoscope from his ears.

"I left for some food and coffee and came back to her on the porch like this. I don't even know who she is. She seems to know Jessie though."

"This is Rina," Cam said. "She's stable, but we need to get her to the hospital.

"Wonder why Jessie never mentioned her."

They strapped Rina to the gurney and prepared to transport her to the hospital. "We're taking her to Methodist Hospital. Do you know where that is?" Cam asked.

"No. What's the address?" AJ punched it into the GPS app on his phone.

As the ambulance pulled away, AJ glanced down at Petey who was looking up at him and whining. "Well, boy, how about I put you in the house and I go check on your mom?" AJ glanced around quickly, hoping no one heard him talking to the dog. Petey walked into the house and headed for the kitchen as if he belonged there. He stopped and scratched at a cupboard door. AJ opened the cabinet and found a bag of dog treats. "I'm guessing these are yours?" He pulled one out and gave it to Petey who was waiting patiently. Holding the treat in his mouth, Petey trotted out into the living room and plopped down on the rug in front of the door to eat it.

"I hope you won't tear up the house. Can I trust you to be good? Great. I'm talking to the dog like he's going to answer." He would have to trust Petey not to tear up the house. With a last look at the dog curled up and sleeping, he locked up and strode over to the truck. Following the directions from his phone, he drove across town to the hospital.

The tiny waiting area for the ER was empty when he arrived. He rushed over to the desk. "Is there any news on Rina Abbott? She was brought in by ambulance." He looked around nervously. Hospitals were definitely not his favorite place to be; so much of his youth was spent in hospitals while they tried to get his asthma under control.

"Are you family?" the nurse at the desk asked.

"Well, no," he replied.

"Then I can't release any information to you. I'm sorry."

Cam walked out of the treatment area and heard her answer. "It's okay. He's Rina's fiancé. He's the one who called 911."

"Cam, you know that doesn't matter. Without a signed HIPAA form, I can't release any information about her condition to him. Now, do you have her insurance card? I need to know who will be responsible for the bill."

"I don't know if she has insurance. Put me down as the responsible party until I can talk to her."

A car screeched to a halt in front of the door, and a man holding a bloody towel on his arm rushed in. "I've got to handle this. Cam, can you take him back?"

"Sure thing, Theresa."

Cam pulled AJ through the doors into the treatment area. "Rina is still out. They won't let you back to see her if you're not family without her okay. I figured fiancé would work."

They arrived at the treatment room, stepping back when the doctor opened the door.

"This is Doctor O'Conner. Doc, this is Jessie's brother AJ", Cam said. "He's the one who found Rina. What's her condition?"

"She has a serious infection that was turning into septicemia due to a wound on her foot that had become infected. We got that cleaned and stitched up, and I put her on IV antibiotics and fluids. She is severely dehydrated."

AJ frowned wondering how she got that sick and no one noticed. "Does she have any family? I just wonder if there is anyone we should call?"

"Just Jessie," Cam answered. "I don't think she has any family. She's never talked about any. Jessie will know if we should call anyone else. I'll call him right now."

"I was going to ask if you knew where he was," AJ said. "I tried to call him last night and this morning and got his voice mail."

"He went camping in the state park. Some areas don't have any cell reception. Maybe he just couldn't get a signal." Cam dialed his cell phone, scowling when he connected with Jessie's voicemail. "Well, I guess we wait until he calls us back." Putting his phone in his pocket, he asked, "Do you know if she has anyone to watch her dogs? Jessie is usually the one who does it when she isn't able to."

"Dogs? She only had one with her when I found her," AJ replied. "How many does she have? I can stop by tonight and make sure they have food and water."

"The one who was with her is Petey. She takes him everywhere. I think she has about twenty dogs right now. She runs a no-kill shelter out of the barn on her property."

"I can handle that. Where does she live?"

"She lives about a mile south down the road from Jessie."

They both looked up when an orderly pushed Rina's gurney out of the treatment room. The nurse followed with the bag containing Rina's clothes, handing it to AJ. He found her keys lying on top of her clothing and hoped the key to the shelter was one of the few on the paw print keychain.

Once Rina was transferred to a regular room, he pulled up a forest green recliner, the vinyl creaking as he settled in to watch over her. With Jessie being MIA for the moment, he felt responsible for her. Why the hell didn't he tell him he had someone in his life? Oh yeah. Sasha, the bitch extraordinaire who drove a wedge between them. Maybe Jessie still harbored some resentment over that misunderstanding. Thoughts of Sasha and Jessie brought up the memories of the day Jessie enlisted in the Marines.

Three years ago at AJ's college graduation party…

The thought of finally being done with school had AJ smiling as he strolled toward the keg. Jessie filled AJ's glass and mentioned making a run to the store for more ice.

AJ pulled his keys out of his pocket. "You might as well take the 'Cuda. I won't be driving anywhere tonight."

Sipping his beer, he stepped out onto the back deck and stared out across the lawn, thinking about the idea he had for a novel. A hand on his arm brought his attention back to the party. He turned and found Jessie's girlfriend, Sasha, looking at him with lust in her eyes.

"I'm not Jessie," he said. "He went to get some more ice, but he should be back any minute."

"Good," she purred as she ran her hand up and down his arm. "I want to see if you are identical in every way." She put her hand behind his head and pulled him down into a kiss, running her other hand across the front of his jeans.

He pushed at her shoulders, trying to extricate himself from her embrace.

"Come on, AJ. I don't care which brother I have."

A hand on his shoulder pulled him back forcefully. "You bastard! Making moves on my girlfriend while I'm off getting ice for your party?" Jessie punctuated his question by punching AJ in the face. "You can have her. I hope you're both happy!" he yelled over his shoulder as he stomped out the door and over to AJ's 'Cuda. Tires squealed and gravel flew as he drove away.

AJ backed away from Sasha. "What the hell, Sasha? I knew you were shallow, but this is insane. Did you really think I would be open to doing it with my brother's girlfriend? Get out of my house, you bitch." He stuck his

11

hand in his pocket to get his keys, forgetting he gave them to Jessie to go make the run for ice.

He tried calling Jessie's cell phone, grimacing when the voice mail prompted him to leave a message. "Come back, Jessie. It's not how it looked… Oh hell, yes it was. Come back so we can talk about this."

AJ sat on the couch and drank beer after beer, staring at his phone and willing it to ring. Some of his friends helped him pick up the worst of the mess after everyone else left. After another futile attempt to contact Jessie, he dropped onto the couch and started snoring.

He woke the next morning to a thumping hangover headache, finding his keys lying in the middle of the table and Jessie's clothes gone. Shit.

It was two years before Jessie contacted him from his hospital bed in Germany. His tibia had been shattered by a bullet when he was on a patrol with his unit. AJ was already at the airport waiting for a flight to California to be with Jessie when he got the call. He was headed to Camp Pendleton, the Marine base where Jessie had been stationed before he shipped out to Afghanistan.

It had taken almost an entire year, but they were finally talking again, and their relationship was almost back to normal. Then the pain came again, and AJ hopped on a plane and headed for Indiana, knowing that Jessie was hurt.

"Jessie?"

He looked up at the soft voice bringing him back to the present with a jolt.

"You're not Jessie," she whispered before she fell back to sleep.

"You better hang on to this one, Jessie," he said to himself. "She can tell us apart when she's not delirious."

He straightened her blanket and turned to walk out of the room, belatedly remembering his promise to Cam to take care of her dogs. Pulling the bag out of the drawer, he fished out her keys and walked out of her room, feeling like he should have stayed and watched over her.

Chapter Three

AJ TRIED to make sense of the few pieces of the puzzle that was Rina. She looked like she hadn't eaten a decent meal in weeks, she loved Jessie, but he left her alone and went camping when she was sick, and she took care of abandoned and mistreated animals. He smiled absently at Petey's frantic barking as he unlocked the front door. Relieved to find the house looked just as he left it, he scratched Petey's ears. "Your mom's doing okay, and she should be home within a couple of days. It's just you and me for a while."

After changing into an old pair of jeans and a t-shirt he found in his brother's dresser, he drove down the road to Rina's property to care for the dogs in the shelter. He could see where Rina had invested money in a large fenced area and some smaller fenced dog runs. The fences looked new, but the barn looked like it had been there for a long time. The classic red paint had worn away in spots showing the faded grey of the weathered siding, and the rusty nails protruding from the siding could have been fixed with a simple hammer.

Unlocking the padlock on the door, he pulled it open and was surprised to find the inside was very clean and modern. The small waiting area held a couple of chairs covered in an industrial-grey fabric separated by a small table and a rack holding a collection of literature. *Wow, I can tell where she spent her money*, he thought. Petey trotted in and immediately went to a dog bed set up in the corner. After circling three times, he plopped down and rested his head on his paws. The small waiting area was filled with all kinds of dog magazines and informational pamphlets scattered around the room on the table and in the rack. He walked past the reception desk and opened the door to the kennels, impressed with the size of the kennels and the general cleanliness of the shelter. He walked up and down the center aisle stopping to meet each of the dogs.

The dogs all looked well cared for and healthy. He stopped at each kennel and read the information card. A lab mix bounced around the kennel, throwing a knotted rope in the air and catching it, a Chihuahua barked non-stop, and a pit bull mix panted at him from the bed in the corner. When he walked up to the last kennel, he discovered a beautiful Australian Shepherd just sitting and looking at him as if to say 'it's about time you showed up'. The dog was grey with darker spots, his face half grey and half black. He couldn't understand how people could discard these animals as if they were yesterday's trash. He checked the info card and discovered his name was Gunner, and he was a Blue Merle. "So, Gunner, how are you today?" he asked as if he expected an answer.

He transferred the dogs to the fenced area, Gunner herding them toward the door as they barked and tussled. Once all the kennels had been cleaned out, he bribed the dogs with treats, brought them in, and returned them to the correct areas one by one. The food was stored in a large plastic bin with the feeding schedule tacked to the wall above it. The repetitive nature of filling the food bowls gave his mind free reign to think about his brother, and the worry made his stomach roll. "Where the hell are you, Jessie?" he asked aloud.

After locking the barn, he checked that the doors on the house were locked. Rina wasn't in her right mind when she started walking over to Jessie's, and he was relieved to find both the front and the back doors closed and locked.

On the way back to Jessie's, Petey rode next to him in the cab of the truck, his head sticking out the window enjoying the smells on the air rushing past. AJ smiled at him. "It's good to have someone to talk to even if you can't answer. It's been lonely living by myself."

After filling the dog bowl he brought back from the shelter, he set it on the kitchen floor and called Petey who came prancing in before AJ stood up. Once the dog started eating, AJ filled another bowl with water and put it down next to the food dish. With Petey's needs taken care of, AJ grabbed clean clothes out of his duffel and closed himself in the bathroom to get cleaned up.

After a shower and a quick sandwich, AJ drove back

to the hospital to check on Rina. Finding her sleeping, he glanced at her chart noting her temperature was going down. *That's a good sign; the antibiotics must be starting to work.* Feeling responsible for her, he plopped down into the chair and opened up his laptop. His glasses on, he opened the manuscript for his most recent project and lost himself in his story of intrigue and murder.

AJ jerked awake. His dreams had been a jumble of searching for his brother lost in the woods and on the battlefields of Afghanistan. He grabbed his laptop, saving it from crashing to the floor.

"Good save."

He looked up and found Rina awake and watching him.

"You must be Bobo."

"Hey. Yeah, I'm Bobo. Actually, it's AJ. Jessie is the only one who calls me Bobo." He set his laptop on the floor. "How are you feeling?"

"How did I get here? The last thing I remember is walking along the creek headed to Jessie's to get a ride to the doctor's office," she said with a yawn. "I saw Jessie drive by in his truck. I figured he was on a coffee run and would be back by the time I got to his place."

"That was me you saw in Jessie's truck. I got back to Jessie's and found you passed out on the front steps. You're lucky I had decided that coffee and groceries were the top priority; otherwise, I might have been gone all day."

"Where's Jessie?"

"I don't know. I was hoping you could tell me," AJ

said, trying to keep the worry out of his voice. "I think he needs help, wherever he is."

He looked over and saw Rina had drifted off again. Wondering why he felt so protective of her, he tried to convince himself it was because she was Jessie's girl-friend, and therefore she was family. His heart twisted at the memory of finding her crumpled on the front porch steps looking so beautiful yet so fragile. She looked even smaller in the hospital bed, reminding him of how thin she had looked in her baggy clothes. He planned to ask the doctor tomorrow if anything else was wrong; the apparent weight loss worried him.

He yawned realizing how tired he was after taking care of Rina's dogs. He wondered if she had anyone helping her. Taking care of the dogs was a lot of work for one person.

His heart pounded from his dream of searching for Jessie as he opened his eyes in the dimly lit hospital room. He looked over at Rina sleeping peacefully, unaware of his presence. Her dark eyelashes against her pale skin just above the curve of her cheek stirred something within him. He briefly thought about staying but then remem-bered Petey would need to go out. Moving the blanket off his lap, he pried himself out of the chair. He walked down the silent hall and stopped at the nurses station. "Thanks for letting me stay," he said, smiling at one of the nurses. "What time does the doctor make rounds in the morning?"

"Be back by nine. I'll let the doctor know you'd like to talk with him."

"Thanks." AJ turned and headed for the elevator.

Petey was waiting patiently by the door when AJ returned to Jessie's. Following the dog out the back door, he leaned against the railing of the deck, watching Petey go from tree to tree to bush, watering each one in turn. "Sorry I left you here by yourself so long today, Petey. I went to see your mom and make sure she's okay, and I fell asleep. She should be back tomorrow." Petey sat at AJ's feet and looked up at him before jumping up into his lap. "You miss her, don't you?" AJ asked as he scratched the dog's ears. "Well, you'll just have to put up with me until she gets back." He stroked Petey's head with one hand as he set the alarm on his phone with the other. "Come on, Petey. I have to be up early, so we better get to bed." Petey jumped down and stood by the door as if telling AJ to hurry up already.

The next morning, AJ strode up to Rina's room just as the doctor walked out and closed the door. Remembering the hospital thought he was Jessie, he walked up and said, "Hey, Doc. What's the prognosis?"

"The antibiotics are working, and her fever is almost gone. She can go home this afternoon," the doctor replied with a smile. "She will have to stay off of that foot until the stitches are removed next week. I'll have a pair of crutches sent up."

"Good. I have some questions. Is there somewhere we can talk?"

Half an hour later, the doctor looked down at his phone as it beeped. "I've got to get back to my rounds."

"Thanks for taking the time to talk with me."

AJ walked down the hall to Rina's room relieved that

the weight loss wasn't from something medical. He was still worried about why it was happening. Maybe she'd tell Jessie when he got back.

After a soft knock, he opened the door to find Rina staring out the window, lost in thought.

She turned at the sound of the door opening. "Hi," she said with a shy smile. "I almost had myself convinced that I dreamt you up."

"Nope. I'm real. Doc says you can go home this afternoon." He watched her face to see her reaction. "I'll be back at about three to pick you up."

"You don't need to do that. I can have Cam drop me off when he gets off work at five. I'm sure you have better things to do than cart me around town," she said as she picked at her nails. "And I want to thank you for taking care of my dogs. You didn't go in the house did you?" she asked, looking relieved when he said no.

"It's the least I could do for my brother's girl," he commented, not noticing the grimace on her face. "Do you have anyone to help you with the dogs? You're not going to be able to do it yourself for a while. Doc says you have to stay off that foot for at least a week."

"I've got it covered." She jumped when her phone rang.

"I'll be back at three," AJ whispered. He started toward the door and glanced over his shoulder to see her pick up her phone and frown at the number on the caller ID.

Chapter Four

RINA STARED at the television as if she were mesmerized by the sitcom it was tuned to, but she wasn't seeing it. All she could see was AJ's emerald green eyes, so like Jessie's but brighter. She was frantically trying to figure out a way to keep her no-kill shelter open, and she was distracted by her best friend's brother. The call from her lawyer earlier in the day was not the news she had been hoping for; someone had frozen all her bank accounts, so she didn't have access to any of her money. The inheritance from her grandfather, her personal savings, and her business accounts were all frozen. Her lawyer indicated he had filed paperwork with the court to get them released, but he couldn't get a court date for a couple of weeks.

The last of her on-hand cash had been spent on dog food and supplies for the shelter two weeks ago. Making sure the dogs were taken care of was her first priority. Her cupboards were almost empty, and she'd been eating one meal a day to make what food she had last longer.

She looked up at the sound of the door opening, smiling at AJ even though her world was falling apart around her.

"You ready to go, Rina?" he asked as he pushed the wheelchair over to the bed.

He helped her into the wheelchair, glaring at her. When she grabbed his arm to keep her balance, it felt like every nerve ending lit up and short-circuited her brain.

As he pushed her toward the front entrance, it occurred to her no one had said anything about her lack of insurance or pressured her about a payment plan. "Wait. I need to stop and make arrangements for the bill." She put her hands down on the wheels to stop them from turning.

"No need. I took care of it earlier today," he admitted. "The last thing you need right now is to be worrying about a hospital bill. Just pay me back when you can."

"You paid the bill? What did you do that for?" she asked, her voice getting louder and louder. "What gave you the right to do that?" She looked away, not wanting him to see the tears building in her eyes. She had worked so hard; she didn't want to give up now.

He ran his hands through his dark brown hair. "I'm sorry. I just wanted to help"

"Please, just take me home."

When they arrived at Jessie's truck, he opened the door and turned around and picked her up out of the wheelchair, setting her down on the seat gently before closing the truck door. Rina watched as he pushed the wheelchair back into the hospital. The nagging voice of her mother started in. *You need a man in your life. Let him take care of you.* She frowned and muttered to herself, "Shut up, Mother. I'm not like you."

AJ climbed into the truck and started it up, grimacing when he ground the gears taking off for home. He turned on the radio to dispel the quiet, a muscle in his jaw twitching as he tried to ignore her. How did she get under his skin so quickly? He made a mental list of where he wanted to search for Jessie to keep his mind off his passenger, but he couldn't get the picture of her crumpled on the porch steps out of his mind.

He pulled up to Rina's house and shut off the truck, steeling himself for the argument that was sure to come. Swinging Rina up into his arms and walking toward her front door, he almost dropped her when she screeched in his ear. "What are you doing? Put me down!"

"No can do, Rina. My mama would roll over in her grave if I let you down now. Let me be a gentleman, please." He strode purposefully toward the house, wanting to get this over with quickly. He opened the door after she leaned over and unlocked it.

"You can put me down now, AJ," she said, looking around frantically. "Thank you for all your help, but I'll be fine from here."

He set her down on the couch in the living room. "Here are your antibiotics. It's time for you to take them. I'll get you a glass of water." He walked into the kitchen, and opening and closing cupboards, he looked for a water glass. Noticing how empty everything looked, he decided he would stop tomorrow and buy her some groceries. If she was going to be pissed at him anyway, he might as well make sure she has some food in the house. He reached over and flipped the switch to turn on the overhead light and scowled when nothing happened. Maybe something popped the breaker. He found the glasses and turned on the water to fill one, and again nothing happened. *What the hell?*

"Rina, you have no water and no electricity. What is going on?" he asked, the concerned look back on his face. "There's no way you can stay here. You are coming with me to Jessie's."

"No way. The electric company just screwed up my bill again. I'll call and have them turn the power back on."

He looked at her and noticed the bills she tried to shove under the couch cushion. He pulled them out and saw they were all stamped "Overdue" or "Last Notice". "What the hell is this?" He continued to go through the stack. "Does Jessie know about this?"

"No, and he won't know about it. I just hit a rough patch, and I'll get it all straightened out soon." She grabbed her crutches and stood. "I'll be fine. You did your duty, so you can go now."

"Not going to happen, Rina. You're staying at Jessie's until this is cleared up." He walked toward the stairs. "Which room is yours? I'll grab some of your clothes, and we can leave."

He returned with a bag full of her clothes and her toiletries and found her still sitting on the couch staring at the fireplace, her eyes unfocused.

"No. I'm not going."

He shook his head at her and took the bag out to the

truck. He came back in and lifted her up in his arms, fighting how touching her affected him.

"Put me down!"

"I'm doing this for your own good. I bet you were going to try and take care of the dogs by yourself, too. Don't worry about them; I'll come back later to clean the kennels and feed them."

He carried her out to the truck, setting her on the seat. "Stay here. I'll be right back." He walked down to the barn, unlocked the side door, and herded the dogs out into the large fenced area.

He returned to the truck after locking the barn. "I'll come back after I get you settled in over at Jessie's to clean the kennels and get them all fed."

She turned away from him as a tear streaked down her cheek.

After setting her on Jessie's couch, he went back out to grab her bag. "I'll put your stuff in Jessie's room since my stuff is already in the guest room." After dropping her bag on Jessie's bed, he handed her the remote for the television. "I'm going to go take care of the dogs. Is there anything you need before I go?"

"No," she said as she turned on the television without looking at him.

She relaxed when she heard the truck pull away. It was a relief to not have to hide her emotions. Sitting in front of the television doing nothing was not how she liked to spend her time, so she hobbled into the kitchen on her crutches. She was determined to find some way to help. The thought of not pulling her weight made her stomach churn. No way would she end up like her mother, dependent on a man for everything. She dug through the fridge and pulled out some hamburger, onion, and tomatoes to make a pot of chili. She could at least cook dinner while he was taking care of her dogs. Every cent she had went to keeping up the shelter, so at least there was electricity and water in the barn until the end of the month. She pulled out the cutting board and set it on the table, sitting down to chop the onion and tomatoes.

AJ returned to find Rina asleep on the couch with Petey curled up next to her. He hoped Jessie would be back soon so he wouldn't be tempted to act on his feelings. He smelled the air, inhaling the scent of the chili, and his stomach rumbled reminding him that lunch had been hours ago. Ambling into the kitchen, he lifted the lid on the pot of chili and sniffed appreciatively as he gave it a stir.

AJ had just turned off the water and stepped out of the shower to dry off when he heard Rina scream. With the towel in his hand, he ran into the living room, his heart slamming into his ribs. He found Rina sleeping on the couch thrashing around and mumbling, "No. Don't hurt her. Leave her alone." Relieved to see she wasn't in danger, he realized he was standing there completely nude. His cheeks burned as he wrapped the towel around his hips and walked over to the couch. Bending over, he laid his hand on her forehead, checking that her fever hadn't returned. At the touch of his hand, Rina quietly sighed. He straightened the blanket covering her and slowly walked back to the bathroom, wondering what in her dream caused such a violent reaction.

After shaving and brushing his teeth, AJ walked out of the bathroom to Rina awake and stirring something in a large bowl with a wooden spoon. She looked up and smiled, making his heart skip a beat.

She's Jessie's. She's Jessie's. She's Jessie's, he thought, trying to get his traitorous heart under control.

"Since you've been so great about taking care of the dogs, I thought I would make you dinner," she said with a small smile. "I feel like it's the least I could do, especially after you paid my hospital bill." She poured the batter out of the bowl into a waiting cake pan. "The cornbread should be done in about fifteen minutes. Could you please carry the dishes and silverware to the table for me? They're too heavy for me to carry one-handed."

He got caught up in her eyes for a moment. "Sure, no problem," he replied, turning and pulling dishes out of the cupboard. Wanting nothing more than to pull her into his arms and hold her close, he started setting the table. "So, how long have you known Jessie?" he asked.

"I moved back here about six months ago. I met Jessie when he helped me round up the dogs after someone cut the fence and they all escaped." She turned and placed the cake pan in the oven. "Why did you come here without knowing if Jessie was even here? Didn't he tell you he was going on one of his camping trips?"

AJ tried to think of an answer that wouldn't make him sound like a complete flake. "I just needed to see him," he replied, not wanting to tell her he thought Jessie was in trouble. He forced himself to put his hand in his pocket to keep from rubbing his leg. "I'm starving. Is that cornbread done yet?" he asked, trying to get the conversation off him and Jessie.

After eating in silence, AJ cleared the table and started to rinse the plates before putting them in the dishwasher. Rina transferred the leftover chili to a bowl, covering it with plastic wrap. When she almost dropped it on the floor, AJ reached over and grabbed the bowl and placed it in the refrigerator.

"I was getting it," she said with a frown.

"I didn't want to be cleaning it up off the floor," he replied as he pulled out a beer. "You want a soda or something?"

"No, thanks. I think I'm just going to go to bed. I'm still not feeling a hundred percent," she said as she slowly made her way toward the bedrooms.

He reached over and placed the back of his hand on her forehead. "You didn't overdo it, did you?"

"No. I'm okay. Just tired," she stammered as she stared at the floor.

He pulled the crutches out of her hands, picked her up, and carried her into Jessie's bedroom. "Why didn't you say something?"

"You've already done so much," she mumbled as he carried her to the bedroom. "I didn't want you to feel like you have to take care of me."

He looked down at her and was mesmerized by her mouth, his eyes lingering on her lips as she spoke.

He gently laid her on the bed, slowly sliding his arm

from behind her back, and dragged his gaze away from hers. He stalked out of the room and returned with her crutches. "Don't worry about the dogs tomorrow. I'll take care of them on my way into town."

"AJ?"

"Do you need something? A glass of water?"

"No. I just wanted to thank you for taking care of me and my dogs. I don't know what would have happened if you hadn't shown up when you did."

"Glad I could help," he said softly. He turned and walked to the doorway before looking back at her with eyes blazing. "Let me know if you need anything from your house. I'll bring it back tomorrow afternoon. Good night."

"Good night, AJ."

AJ stared at the old western playing on the television just to have some background noise as he thought about the events of the last two days. Why is it that he finally found a woman that stirred something in him and she had to be Jessie's?

Rina sat on the bed in shock, trying to figure out what had just happened. For a moment, she thought he was going to kiss her, but all he did was tell her not to worry about her dogs. And where did he get the idea that she was Jessie's girlfriend? She changed into the oversized t-shirt she normally wore to bed and crawled under the covers wondering why AJ was there and why he was acting so strangely.

Chapter Five

RINA AWOKE the next morning to find AJ gone. He left a note with his cell number telling her to text him if there was anything she needed that he could pick up at her house or in town. Apprehensive of trying to take a shower balancing on one foot, she filled the tub for a bath. She relaxed, letting the hot water soak away some of her stress. Unfortunately, it would take more than a hot bath to fix the mess her life was in right now.

She sat up when she heard the front door slam and AJ calling her name. Sitting herself on the edge of the tub, she swung her legs around, grabbing the towel bar to help keep her balance while she stood. The bathroom door flew open, and AJ stood there staring at her, chest heaving as if he'd just run a sprint. She grabbed a towel off of the towel bar, wrapping it around herself.

"What the hell, AJ?"

"Why didn't you answer your phone? I've been calling for half an hour!" he yelled, his eyes shining bright as emeralds. He took a quick step forward and brushed a stray curl off her face before lowering his head and slamming his lips on hers.

The world seemed to stand still when his lips touched hers. When he finally pulled away, Rina was glad she still had her hand on the towel bar; otherwise, she might have ended up in a heap at his feet. She smiled up at him, and it was as if someone flipped a switch. His worried eyes narrowed in an instant as anger hardened his face. He ran his hand through his hair, looking like he was going say something, but he turned and stalked out of the bathroom. She heard the front door slam a moment later.

What the hell was that all about? she wondered. After dressing and rewrapping her foot, she picked up her cell phone and saw five missed calls while she had been in the bathall from AJ. She checked her settings and realized she had it set to vibrate. Well, that explained why she didn't hear the phone but not why AJ reacted the way he did.

AJ sped down the road, gritting his teeth to keep himself from yelling. When he had called the third time and she still didn't answer, he had started to panic. What if she fell and hit her head? Or what if she had a relapse? Or what if… By that time, he could only think of finding her and making sure she was safe. He pulled off the road into the McDonald's parking lot, needing to calm himself down before he did something stupid like fall for Jessie's girlfriend. He scrubbed his face with his hands as he realized it was too late; he had already fallen for her. *I better find Jessie quickly*, he thought, *before I do something that ruins our relationship forever.*

After a few minutes, he pulled out of the parking lot and drove toward the state park to talk to the rangers, hoping one of them knew where Jessie was camping. AJ rubbed his leg firmly, the increase in pain furrowing his brow. He looked at the dog tags hanging from the rear-view mirror, reminding him of the pain Jessie went through eighteen months ago when he was shot.

"The bullet shattered his tibia, and we thought we might have to amputate at one point. But Jessie's a fighter, and my team worked tirelessly to save his leg. He may be left with diminished use of the leg. Perhaps a limp or weakness. You can go in and see him."

"Thanks, Doc," AJ said, shaking the doctor's hand.

He walked into Jessie's hospital room to find his brother lying in bed, his leg propped up and heavily wrapped in white bandages. Jessie's face fought to stay indifferent, but AJ knew he was glad he had come to be with him.

The pain this time wasn't the same as when Jessie was shot, but it still worried him. Finding Jessie had to be his priority.

An hour later, he walked out of the ranger station at the state park no closer to finding Jessie than he was yesterday. Jessie never camped in the same place twice, and the rangers hadn't seen him. Heading back to town, he decided to stop by the fire station and see if Cam was working; maybe he had some ideas about where Jessie was camping this time.

Seeing the ambulance sitting at the fire station, he pulled into the parking lot behind the building. Cam walked out and did a double take as AJ approached him. "Hey, man. I thought you were going to be camping until next week."

He noticed the expression on Cam's face change as he walked closer.

"Sorry, man. I thought you were Jessie back early. Damn. How did your mama tell you two apart?"

"Sometimes she didn't," AJ replied. "Can I ask you a question, Cam?"

"Sure. Hey, how's Rina doing?"

"She's doing great. I'll let her know you asked about her." AJ stopped and tried to formulate a way to ask about Jessie's campsite without giving away why he wanted to know. "Do you know where Jessie was planning on camping this time? I thought I'd join him for a few days."

"Sorry, man. Jessie always keeps his campsites a secret. You know he doesn't like unwanted visitors while he's doing his nature thing."

"I guess I'll just wait for him to get back then. Thanks anyway." AJ shook Cam's hand and turned to go back to his truck.

"You're worried about him, aren't you?" Cam asked as AJ started to walk away.

"Yeah, I am. How did you know?"

"You get the same look on your face when you're worried that Jessie does. It's spooky how much you two look alike." Cam turned to go. "I'll let you know if I hear from him."

"Thanks, Cam. Appreciate it," AJ said before striding

back toward Jessie's truck. *Damn. Can't catch a break*, he thought as he started the truck.

Rina spent the day watching television. Well, channel surfing really. She just couldn't figure AJ out. He talked about her being Jessie's girlfriend, and then he laid a scorching hot kiss on her. And they say women are moody…

Chapter Six

THE BREEZE RUFFLED AJ's hair as he sat in the truck in front of Rina's barn and thought about his lack of progress in finding his brother. He was no closer to finding Jessie than he was when the cab dropped him off. Every time he tried Jessie's phone, the call went directly to voice mail. After the third call, he quit leaving voice messages; it was obvious Jessie wasn't getting them or he was ignoring them. "Dammit, Jessie. Where the hell are you?" AJ grumbled as if someone would answer out of thin air. After talking to Cam, he went to the sheriff's office and tried to get some help there, but that was a bust also. Since Jessie wasn't due back until the next week, he wasn't officially missing.

Resigned to holding off on his search for Jessie until tomorrow, AJ climbed out of the truck and went into the barn to take care of the dogs. The mindless work of cleaning kennels and filling food dishes helped calm his mind. He gave all the dogs some attention, but he had taken a special liking to the beautiful, grey Australian Shepherd, Gunner. Knowing he couldn't save them all, he decided he could at least save Gunner. A talk with Rina about adopting the pup would be his first order of business when he returned to Jessie's. The feel of the dog's fur beneath his fingers seemed to take his mind off of everything going on, at least for a few minutes. Truly relaxed for the first time since the pain hit, he decided it was time to talk to Cam and tell him why he was worried about Jessie, hoping he could help him search the state park.

After filling all the water dishes, AJ turned out the lights and locked up the barn, his mind whirling with thoughts of Rina, his brother, and whether he should tell Rina why he was in Woodview. Considering why she was staying at Jessie's, he decided not to tell her, not yet anyway. She had enough on her mind already. AJ couldn't believe Jessie had let her live in her house alone with no water or electricity.

AJ walked in the front door to find Rina in the kitchen pulling some chicken out of the oven. His stomach rumbled, reminding him that lunch had been hours ago. "Hey, Rina. You know I don't expect you to cook every night. You're supposed to be taking it easy and staying off that foot," he said as he walked over to the sink and washed his hands.

"I know. I want to do it. And for your information, I was riding the couch all day." She transferred green beans from a pan to a bowl. "If you can carry the food to the table, we can eat," she said as she set the chicken on a platter before hobbling over to the table to sit down.

Once they filled their plates and started eating, Rina asked about the dogs, obviously concerned about their care. "I got a call about three more dogs that are scheduled to be put down. Would you mind taking me to pick them up? I can't stand to think of any being put down for a lack of responsible owners."

AJ watched her face as she talked about the dogs and was impressed with the conviction of her beliefs. "Actually, I wanted to talk to you about Gunner. We seem to have clicked, and I want to adopt him."

She looked up with the biggest smile lighting up her face. "Really? That is the best news!"

Her smile destroyed his intentions to stay away from her. "Yes, really." He gathered up their plates and placed them in the sink after dumping the chicken bones in the trash. "Just let me know what paperwork I need to fill out. I'll bring him back here after I clean the kennels in the morning."

"Let's go get him tonight. I need to see all the dogs anyway." She blushed. "Not that I don't think you're taking great care of them… I just miss them."

"Sure, on one condition. You let me take a look at your foot first. I want to make sure it's not getting infected again." He cleared the rest of the dishes from the table and placed them on the counter. "Now, you cooked, so I'll clean up. Go sit down, and I'll check your foot in a few minutes."

Rina lounged on the sofa waiting for AJ to finish up the dishes so he could look at her foot.

Once he had everything set out, he pulled a pair of

glasses out of his pocket and put them on before he unwrapped the bandages.

Rina swallowed trying to find her voice. The sight of AJ in those glasses did something to her. She felt like she had melted into a puddle on the floor. She cleared her throat. "So, what do you do when you're not rescuing damsels in distress?" *Damsels in distress? What am I, twelve?*

He looked up at her, and her stomach did a slow somersault.

"I actually teach high school creative writing." His attention returned to her foot as he continued. "And I'm a published author."

"Wow. That is so cool. What do you write? Maybe I've read it." Her face burned as she looked at her hands. She couldn't believe she had just gushed like a teenager over the latest boy band.

"I write mysteries under the name Monroe Jackson. The first was released about six months ago." She surmised the stitches must have looked okay from the look of relief of his face.

"No. I haven't read it. I'll make sure to look for it when my accounts get released," she said, belatedly realizing what she just let slip. Luckily, AJ seemed to be concentrating on her foot and wasn't listening. His hand was resting on her foot, and it felt like the bandages should have caught fire.

"I don't see any sign of infection. If we can keep you off that foot, I think it will heal just fine." He grabbed sterile pads and gauze out of the first aid kit and rewrapped her foot.

She reluctantly pulled her foot out of his lap and stood. "Let's go get Gunner so you can come back and take a shower. I'm sure you're tired," she said, trying to cover up what the sight of him in a pair of glasses had done to her.

When they pulled up to the barn, they saw the door was open, and the light was on. "Stay in the truck," AJ said, grabbing the tire iron out from under the seat. "I know I locked up and turned all the lights off when I left."

He walked slowly into the barn, feeling relieved when it looked like all the dogs were fine and nothing was missing. Returning to the truck, he helped Rina get her crutches. "Nothing looks disturbed. I must have left it like this. I'm so sorry."

Rina suspected he locked everything up. This had happened a few times over the last couple of months. Someone was trying to scare her off. She had her suspicions but no proof. "It's okay. I shouldn't be expecting you to take care of my dogs. I'll see if I can get someone else out here to do it tomorrow."

"There's no need. I just have a lot on my mind," he said as he walked to the last kennel on the right. "Hi, Gunner. How you doing, boy?" He unlocked the kennel. Gunner trotted out and sat in front of AJ as if he knew they were there to take him home. After bending down to scratch Gunner behind his ears and ruffle his fur, AJ attached the leash in his hand to Gunner's collar. He glanced over to find Rina surrounded by dogs, trying to pet all of them at the same time while keeping her balance on one foot. He handed her Gunner's leash and picked her up.

"AJ, what are you doing? Put me down," she demanded.

He searched around the room for a chair. Spotting the stool over by the cabinets, he carried her over and set her down on it.

"Can't have you putting any weight on that foot." He called the dogs over to her.

Rina couldn't decide if he was doing it because he cared or because he thought she was Jessie's girlfriend. Oh well. She'd worry about that later. Right now, she had some dogs to love on. They were all well behaved, albeit a little rambunctious, sitting and waiting for their turn with their tails wagging.

While Rina was occupied with the dogs, AJ continued to look for anything out of place. He was sure he'd turned off the lights and locked the door. He was definitely going to have a talk with Jessie about it when he decided to show up. Something about the situation stunk like week-old fish, and AJ was afraid Rina was in danger.

He took Gunner outside to see how the pup reacted to being on a leash. Gunner had obviously had some training; he knew how to heel perfectly. "Good job, Gunner!" AJ praised him and scratched his ears. "Let's go see if Rina's ready to go yet."

He walked into the barn to find Rina putting the last dog in their kennel. "You ready to go, Rina?" He smiled at her yawn and handed her Gunner's leash. "Here, take

Gunner and go get in the truck. I'll make sure everything is locked up securely."

Ten minutes later, they were back at Jessie's. Gunner and Petey sat side by side in front of the couch crunching on dog biscuits and getting reacquainted.

"Is there anything else you need, Rina? If you don't, I'm going to take a shower and then go to bed."

"No. I'm good. Thank you for taking care of my dogs, AJ. It means more than you know." She retreated to Jessie's bedroom and shut the door.

AJ sighed and trudged toward the bathroom, wishing things were different. Wishing that she was his girlfriend instead of Jessie's. As the pounding water washed the stress of the day away, he wondered why she provoked such protective feelings in him. Maybe he just wanted what Jessie had…

Chapter Seven

HE SEARCHED the woods for Jessie, knowing he was out there somewhere. The sun dropped below the horizon, ushering in twilight, and he knew he had to find him that night. The whistling of the wind played tricks, rustling leaves that sounded like whispers of far-off voices telling him he was too late.

AJ opened his eyes to the grey wall of Jessie's guest bedroom as the dense forest of his dream drifted further and further away. He ran a shaking hand through his hair and tried to breathe slowly to calm his racing heart. He hadn't had one of the searching dreams for almost a year; when Jessie was in the military and they weren't speaking, he had two or three a week. It had been more than three days since the pain in his leg began, and increasing worry about his brother had seeped into his subconscious, reviving the dreams once again.

Knowing from past experience that it would be at least an hour until he could relax enough to fall asleep again, he pulled on a pair of sweatpants, almost yelling in surprise when a wet dog nose pushed its way into his hand. "Hey, Gunner," he said as he ruffled the dog's fur. "Want to hang out for a while?"

He walked out of the bedroom with Gunner following closely behind. Opening the door to Jessie's room, he looked in on Rina, resisting the urge to walk closer to the bed. He continued on his late-night mission to occupy his mind until the memory of the dream faded enough for him to return to sleep. In the kitchen, AJ filled the water bowls and then reached into the cupboard above the stove for the bottle of whiskey he knew would be there. Dropping a couple ice cubes in a glass, he poured himself a drink, just enough to help him relax.

A soft 'woof' drew his attention to the dog's food dishes. Petey sat and waited patiently for AJ to notice him. "How about a treat, guys?" he asked softly, careful not to wake Rina. Treats in hand, he smiled as Petey performed his repertoire of tricks–sit, shake, down. Gunner sat calmly as if he was too good to do such silly tricks.

Tossing treats to both canines, he walked to the couch without bothering to turn on any lights. Gunner hopped up and lay down next to him as Petey jumped up and snuggled into his lap. Resting his hand on Gunner's head, he took a sip of his drink and closed his eyes while laying his head back on the couch, trying to clear his mind.

He heard a small noise behind him, somehow knowing it was Rina. "Did I wake you?" he asked as he opened his eyes. His heart beat faster as she sat next to him, propping her crutches against the back of the couch. Her hair was all tousled, and she stifled a yawn as she blinked sleepily.

"No. I woke up when Petey jumped off the bed," she replied, trying to sweep her hair out of her face. "What's wrong?"

"Just a dream. You should go back to bed." He took another sip of his drink.

"No. I'll just sit here with you for a while." She scooched in closer to him and rested her head on his arm.

AJ lifted his arm and pulled her in closer to him, letting her rest her head on his chest. He held her close, reveling in the feeling of her as he mentally kicked himself for letting her get this close. He could tell when she dropped into sleep as her head sunk deeper into his chest. Only then did he turn his head and bury his nose in her hair, breathing in the scent that was all Rina–light and fresh like a spring morning. He kissed her hair and let her nearness wash over him.

AJ woke to the smell of coffee and bacon. He hoisted himself off the couch, deciding he'd have to find time for a run before all this home cooking caught up with him. Yawning and stretching, he ambled to the kitchen. "Morning, Rina. I told you cooking for me isn't necessary, but I'm not going to complain."

"Help yourself to some coffee. Breakfast will be done in a minute," she said as she stirred the eggs in the skillet. "Can you let the dogs in and give them some food?"

After getting the dogs in and filling their food dishes, he returned to the table to find a plate of scrambled eggs and bacon waiting for him. Rina was at the stove plating up the rest of the food onto her dish. He watched as she used one crutch and carried her food over to the table.

After eating all the eggs on her plate, Rina looked up and asked, "When are you going to tell me why you are here? I can tell you're worried about Jessie. Why?"

AJ ran his hands through his hair. "You're right. I am worried about him. We've had this connection since we were little. It's a twin thing, I guess. When he was shot in the leg in Afghanistan, I felt pain in my leg. It wasn't the first time I had felt what he felt. Last week, I felt pain in my leg again. I was worried about him, so I came here looking for him." He stood and gathered the empty dishes and placed them in the sink. "It's just a feeling, but I can't shake it," he said, rinsing the dishes and putting them in the dishwasher. He turned to face her, leaning against the counter with his arms crossed over his chest.

"Is it bad?" she asked, her brow furrowed. "Should we call someone?"

"It's not as bad as when he was shot. I'm more worried about him not answering his phone." He returned to his chair at the table, taking her hand in his. "Jessie isn't one to ignore voice mails even when he's off on his camping trips. Cam mentioned Jessie was planning to be gone until Tuesday, so even if we notify the authorities, they won't consider him missing until at least Wednesday." He rubbed his thumb over the back of her hand. "Don't worry. I'll find him before then."

He got up and retrieved the coffee pot, pouring more of the brew into their mugs.

"So, I told you why I'm here. When are you going to

tell me why your electricity was turned off and you had no food in the house?"

Rina looked down at her hands and picked at her thumbnail. "I told you. They just screwed up my account. I'll call them and get it straightened out today." She stood and reached for her crutches. "I need to spend the day at the shelter and take care of paperwork. What time are you heading over there?"

He frowned at her explanation; the pile of bills she had tried to hide from him painted a different picture. He was determined to get her to tell him the truth soon. "Can you be ready in about half an hour?"

Forty minutes later, they pulled up to the barn. AJ jumped out of the truck, still trying to figure out how he could get her to tell him what was really going on. "I'll get the kennels cleaned out, and then I'm going to head for the state park. I have to look for Jessie. I need to be doing something to find him."

After cleaning out all the kennels and making sure all the dogs had food and water, he poked his head into Rina's office, finding her grimacing at her computer screen.

"I'm ready to leave," he said. His breath caught in his chest when she looked up and smiled at him. "Do you need anything before I go? I'll be back by five to pick you up." That smile got to him, and jealousy filled his mind. *She loves Jessie. She loves Jessie.*

"No. I'm good. Thanks, AJ." She turned her attention back to her computer.

As he walked out to the truck with Rina's smile on his

mind, he dialed Cam's cell number, hoping he had the day off so they could both look for Jessie. "Hey, Cam. You working today? ... No?" He opened the truck door, and Gunner jumped in. "I'm going over to the state park to look for Jessie. I could really use your help." He turned the key and started the truck. "Great. I'll pick you up in about ten minutes."

Chapter Eight

AJ WALKED out of the ranger's station at the state park south of town no closer to finding his brother than when he walked in. Jessie had not filed an open fire permit, so he could be camped anywhere. Cam straightened up from where he'd been leaning on the front fender of the truck as he watched Gunner sniff the parking lot.

"Well, he didn't get a permit, and they haven't seen him. I've got a map of the park," AJ said, climbing into the truck. "Let's drive all the roads and see if we can find Jessie's SUV. If we find that, we might be able to find his campsite."

Two hours later, they were poring over the map, trying to decide which direction to go next. AJ chose to go west toward the far side of the park, knowing that Jessie liked to be off by himself. The road turned to dirt, and AJ had a feeling they were going the right way. The dust flew behind them as they continued down the road until AJ slammed on the breaks. Jessie's SUV was parked on the side of the road. "I knew it!" AJ exclaimed. "Now, let's find his campsite."

AJ grabbed a couple water bottles from the cooler and tossed one to Cam before pouring some water for Gunner. Spreading the map out on the hood of the truck, he looked for the obvious places that Jessie would make camp. "Jessie likes to fish, so let's try down by the river," he said, pointing to the map.

They hiked through the woods, the sound of rushing water growing louder the farther they walked into the trees. When they stopped at the river bank, AJ spotted the top of a tent. "Jessie! Jessie!" he bellowed, running toward the tent.

The campsite was laid out with military precision. "This is Jessie's tent, but it looks like no one has been here in a couple of days. "Jessie!" he yelled, looking around as his heart sank. "Looks like he hasn't been here for a while." His chest tightened in panic at the emptiness of the camp. "Jessie!" He listened for an answer.

Gunner barked and pulled at his leash. AJ let Gunner take the lead, wondering if the dog heard something they couldn't. Gunner led them upstream, pulling harder and harder the farther they went. AJ stumbled over an exposed tree root and dropped the leash. Gunner bolted out of sight. Running full out, AJ skidded to a stop at the familiar voice.

"Gunner! What are you doing out here?"

Gunner barked as if telling AJ to hurry up. He jogged around the boulder in front of him to find his brother sitting on a stump, fending off Gunner's exuberant kisses.

Jessie looked up. "About time you showed up, Bobo."

"What the hell, Jessie?" AJ said as he walked up to Jessie. "What happened?" Relieved that Jessie seemed to be in one piece, he pulled his brother into a hug. "Why the hell didn't you call?"

"I lost my cell phone in the river when I slipped. I banged my knee up pretty good, and I've been making my way back to my campsite. Thanks for coming for me, Bro."

AJ pulled out his cell phone, grateful he had enough bars to make a call this far out in the middle of nowhere. He dialed and waited as it rang on the other end. "Rina, we found him. He's okay. Just a banged up knee," he said, smiling wider at Rina's reaction. He held his phone out to Jessie. "She wants to talk to you."

AJ ambled back toward the campsite, wanting to give Jessie some privacy to talk with Rina. Now that he knew Jessie was okay, he started to feel something else: anger. Anger that Rina was living without electricity and water, anger that she obviously hadn't been eating, anger that Jessie had let it happen. He turned and saw Jessie was done on the phone.

Picking up Gunner's leash, AJ walked toward Jessie. "C'mon, Cam. Let's get Mr. Graceful here to the hospital so he can get this knee taken care of." Putting Jessie's arms over their shoulders, they slowly hiked back to the waiting truck.

After helping Jessie to the truck, Cam turned and said, "You go ahead and take him to the hospital. I'll stay and pack up his campsite and drive his SUV back for you."

Jessie pulled Cam into a hug. "Thanks for helping my little brother find me, man."

"Can you take Gunner back to Rina's? I'll pick him up there when we get done at the hospital." AJ handed the end of the leash to Cam at his nod.

"Sure, AJ. See you guys later," Cam said with a wave before turning back toward the campsite.

After maneuvering the truck to get it turned around, AJ took off down the road. The dust had barely begun to kick up behind them when AJ let his pent up anger break through. "What the hell, Jessie? How could you let her live like that? What the hell is the matter with you?" he growled, his knuckles white from the tight grip he had on the steering wheel. "She could have died if I hadn't shown up when I did!"

"What the hell are you talking about, Bobo?" Jessie asked. "Who are you talking about?"

"I'm talking about your girlfriend," AJ said through gritted teeth. *My brother can't be that clueless, can he?* "The cut on her foot got infected. She was almost septic when I found her." He had to stop and compose himself.

"But she's not"

"There's really no excuse."

"Wait a minute. What do you mean by 'let her live like that'? What the hell are you talking about?"

"Her water and electricity have been shut off, and she has a stack of overdue bills. How could you not have known? Dammit. She looked like she hadn't had a decent meal in weeks."

"I knew she was having some trouble with someone

trying to shut down her shelter, but she never said anything about needing money," Jessie said with a frown. "She had an inheritance she was using to fund the shelter, and she had a job at the café in town to take care of her other bills. She should have had plenty of money."

Gritting his teeth to stop himself from saying something he might regret later, he focused on the road in front of him.

It was almost six o'clock when Rina heard Jessie's truck pull into the parking lot in front of the shelter. Gunner ran to the truck, barking to let everyone know someone was there. Bending down to ruffle Gunner's fur, AJ said to the dog, "You did well today, Gunner."

Rina hobbled out the door as fast as she could. She dropped her crutches and threw her arms around Jessie. "Don't ever worry me like that again!"

Jessie grimaced when he put his full weight on his injured knee to keep his balance. "I'm okay. Just a banged up knee. Nothing to be worried about."

AJ shuffled back to the truck, calling for Gunner to jump in. "I'll leave you two alone. See you back at the house."

They both watched as AJ shot down the drive toward the road.

Jessie looked down at Rina. "So, I think you have some explaining to do, Rina. First, why does AJ think you're my girlfriend?"

"I have no idea why he thinks I'm your girlfriend. Two days ago, I woke up in the hospital, and there he was acting all pissed off at me for some reason. I guess the cut on my foot was worse than I thought, and it got infected. I saw AJ driving your truck and thought he was you, so I went to your house to ask you to drive me to get my foot looked at, and I passed out on your porch. AJ found me."

"Why didn't you tell me about the cut on your foot? I could have helped you with the dogs until it healed. Instead, it almost killed you."

She didn't want to explain why she couldn't accept anyone's help, so she ignored his comment, bringing the conversation back to AJ. "I don't know why everyone says you look alike. I really don't see it." She hoped that would get him off the subject so she wouldn't have to talk about her money issues. She knew he'd offer to pay her bills, but she just couldn't accept money from him.

Trying to stay balanced on one foot, she moved to bend down to pick up her crutches, and Jessie grabbed her arm to steady her.

"Dammit. He wasn't kidding. What is really going on, Rina? How much weight have you lost?

Rina tried to ignore the look of concern on his face. "Just a small cash flow problem. I've got it handled," she replied as she bent down and picked up her crutches. "No need for you to worry." Hobbling back into the barn, she left him to stare after her.

Jessie glared up at the cloudless sky, trying to keep his temper in check. No need for him to worry? Like that would stop him from worrying about her unpaid bills and why she was so determined to do things on her own. Looking back at his interactions with her over the last month, he realized the clues had been there: she had kept him out of her house and hadn't offered to cook for him. Normally, they shared meals at her house a couple times a week. He'd been so wrapped up in his own life and planning his camping trip, he'd let a lot of things slide that he normally would have questioned. Limping over to the bench by the door, he sat down and sighed at the relief of getting off his bad leg.

Exhausted from his adventure, he dozed as he listened to the dogs barking inside the shelter and Rina's admonishments to them to cool it. The slam of a car door woke him. He opened his eyes to find Cam grinning at him and his friend Tom standing by Cam's car. "Well, it must not be too bad if they let you go."

"Just stretched some tendons. It'll heal in a week or so."

Cam handed the keys to Jessie. "Glad you're okay, Jess. Stop by the station tomorrow and tell me the whole story. Right now, I feel like I came in halfway through a movie."

"Sure will, Cam. Thanks for bringing my truck by. Appreciate it. You, too, Tom," Jessie said as they climbed into Cam's car. He waved as they took off.

The screech of the screen door brought his attention to Rina staring at the plume of dust left by Cam's car.

"You look exhausted, Rina. Let's get you back to the house. You look like you could fall asleep standing up."

After checking on the dogs one last time, she carefully locked up and clomped over to Jessie's SUV. Jessie watched as she heaved herself up into the seat, trying to figure out why she kept the truth from him.

"You know you're going to have to tell me what's going on, don't you?" he asked as he put the truck in reverse and backed up to turn around. "I can tell it's more than a cash flow problem. Maybe I can help."

"Just drop it, Jess," she said tiredly. "I'll talk to you about it tomorrow. I just need to eat and get some sleep." She stared out the windshield as if she were already trying to figure out a way to not tell him.

After a silent ride back to his house, they both slowly limped their way up the porch steps and through the front door. Jessie closed the door behind them, grateful to be home in one piece.

Rina turned to make her way to the bedrooms. "I'll get my stuff out of your room and sleep on the couch."

"Rina, you need real sleep in a real bed. I'll take the couch," he stated. "I insist."

Intent on the sleeping arrangements, neither one of them heard AJ walk into the room.

"No. I'll take the couch. I'm the only one who hasn't been sick or injured. I already moved your things to the guest room, Rina," AJ said, effectively putting an end to the discussion. "I stopped and got some subs for dinner. I imagine you're both as hungry as I am."

After they finished eating, they watched a movie. The tension was obvious. AJ was fighting his feelings for Rina, Rina was worrying about her money problems, and Jessie was trying to figure out why AJ thought Rina was his girlfriend.

AJ turned off the television when the movie credits started rolling across the screen. Without a word, he locked himself in the bathroom, and they heard him turn on the shower.

Jessie looked at Rina. "Go to bed, Rina. We'll talk tomorrow."

He limped to his bedroom, shutting the door and dropping onto the bed.

The more he thought about it, the more he wanted to let AJ think Rina was his for a while longer. He never thought of Rina in that way before. Maybe he should start.

Chapter Nine

LATER THAT WEEK, Rina was at the doctor's office getting the stitches out of her foot.

"I want you to stay off that foot as much as possible for the next week. If the pain gets worse or it starts looking infected, I want you back here immediately," the doctor said as he pushed the tray of instruments out of the way.

"I'll keep an eye on it this time. I promise," she replied, putting on her shoe. Limping her way out into the waiting room, she found AJ and Jessie laughing with the receptionist. Staring at the two of them, she wondered how everyone thought they looked exactly alike. She could tell the difference between them with no problem.

"You guys ready to go? I'm excited to go and take care of my dogs on my own for a change." She smiled at the identical looks of consternation on both of their faces.

"You don't want to overdo it, Rina." Jessie took her hand and led her out of the building and toward his truck.

He looked over at AJ. "You're better with engines than I am, AJ, so how about you see if you can figure out what's wrong with Rina's van. Rina and I will stay at the house."

"Okay," AJ replied, rolling his eyes at his brother's back.

When they returned to Jessie's, Rina told AJ the keys to the van were in the middle desk drawer and to call if anything needed replaced. She watched as AJ drove off in Jessie's SUV, wondering why he always scowled when she tried to flirt with him.

At the shelter, AJ was dismayed to find the door unlocked again. After a careful check, everything looked as it should, and he took the van keys out of the desk drawer, hoping he could fix her vehicle.

The van, a 1970's delivery vehicle, wouldn't start. The carburetor was bone dry, prompting him to check the fuel filter. Pulling off the part, he discovered it was full of grit. Someone had poured sand in the gas tank. *So much for a simple fix. Why the hell would someone do this to her?* Then he remembered Jessie had mentioned she had some trouble with someone trying to get her shelter closed down.

Dropping onto the bench, he called Jessie. "Hey, Jess. I figured out the problem. Someone put sand in the gas tank." He held his phone away from his ear as Jessie let loose with a string of curses that would make a sailor blush. "It will cost more than the van is worth to fix it."

"Well, I know she won't let me buy her a new one. Go ahead and get the parts to fix it, and I'll tell her the carburetor needs to be rebuilt or something. That way she won't wonder why it's taking so long to fix it."

They ended the call, and AJ drove to town to get the parts he needed.

Back at the house, Jessie walked out on the back deck, appreciating the sight of Rina in a pair of shorts and a tank top. He was happy to see she seemed to be gaining back some of the weight she had lost. Now, if he could just get her to tell him the truth.

"Good news, Rina. AJ can fix your van, but it will take a couple of days. He needs to rebuild the carburetor, so he has to order some parts. You should have wheels again soon."

When she smiled, it occurred to him he hadn't seen her truly smile in quite some time, making him even more determined to get to the truth.

"That's great news! I know it's an old van, but it's all I've got." She wrapped her arms around him and hugged him.

He bent over to bring his lips in contact with hers. Although it felt nice, it was not the physical reaction he had been looking for.

Rina stepped back. "What was that for? Sorry, Jessie, but I don't have those kinds of feelings for you. Did I do something to make you think I did?"

"No." He laughed. "I just thought I would see if there was anything there. I thought maybe we were giving off signals or something that made AJ think you are my girlfriend."

"Oh, okay. You are both nuts."

From the kiss, it was clear to Jessie that Rina was not meant to be his girlfriend. There was no spark. He decided to let AJ think she was his for just a while longer though, looking forward to seeing him squirm.

AJ returned to the shelter with the parts he needed to fix Rina's van. He found the door unlocked, and this time, he knew he locked it before he left. He searched through all the rooms and didn't find anything out of place or missing.

He noticed it was time for the dogs to be fed. He figured he could get that done and let the dogs out into the fenced area for some exercise before he started tearing the van's engine apart. Gunner watched as he filled the food dishes from the open bag of food. He had just set the first dish in the first kennel when Gunner started barking, alerting him to a car pulling up to the building. Walking to the open door, he watched Jessie and Rina get out of the SUV.

He pulled his brother over to the counter. "It happened again. I know I locked up before I left, but when I got back, the door was unlocked. She needs a security system. Someone is walking in and out as if they own the place."

He turned to pick up another dish of food when he heard Rina yell for help. His heart thumped in fear as he ran to find her kneeling in the first kennel, sobbing.

"What is it? What's wrong?" he asked as he put his hand on her back. He looked down and saw the dog he fed was convulsing. "Oh shit! Come on, Rina. We have to get him to the vet."

He looked around, finally seeing Jessie walking in

from the dog runs. "Jessie, we've got a sick dog, and it looks bad. I just fed him, so there might be something wrong with the food." He grabbed a bag and scooped some of the food into it so it could be tested. "Make sure that food gets sealed up and away from the dogs."

He pulled a blanket out of the supply closet and gently picked up the dog. The pup was still, listless, and panting. He ran out to Jessie's SUV and handed the dog to Rina after she climbed in. After buckling up, he took off, the tires squealing as he headed for the nearest vet.

An hour later, the vet came over to talk to them. "The dog is going to be okay. Your quick thinking probably saved him. We tested the food you brought in and found it was laced with rat poison."

Rina turned to AJ, the look of horror on her face making him want to lock her in a box and protect her from the world. He pulled her into his arms and held her, willing his strength into her to help her face the truth: someone wanted to close her shelter and had no problem killing defenseless animals to do it.

"I'll get an alarm system installed today. This will not happen again, Rina." He could see she wanted to refuse citing the fact she couldn't afford a system.

She shuddered. "Okay. I'll do anything to protect my dogs," she said, giving in to him without an argument. "As soon as I get the money, I'll pay you back."

He wanted to insist it wasn't necessary, but the look on her face stopped him. For some reason, she didn't want to accept help, monetary or otherwise. He'd been waiting for her to refuse his help with the dogs now that she was off the crutches.

"We better get back to the shelter. We can stop and get some more food on the way," he said as they walked back to the SUV. "We need to let the sheriff know what is going on. This is a clear case of animal cruelty and breaking and entering."

"I know, but the sheriff doesn't seem to like me. I had him out after the fence was cut, but he said he couldn't do anything about it."

They stopped at the only pet store in town and picked up ten bags of dog food, enough to feed the dogs for at least a week. They pulled into the drive at Rina's and found a county sheriff's car sitting in front of the barn next to Jessie's truck. They hurried into the shelter and heard Jessie arguing with the deputy.

"What do you mean this isn't serious enough to write up? Are you really telling me that?"

AJ could see by the look in Jessie's eyes that this was not going to end well unless he intervened quickly. "Hey, Jess, why don't you go take a walk." Standing right up to Jessie's face, he said, "Taking a swing at a cop will not help the situation. Go cool off."

Jessie stalked off. "Prick," he muttered under his breath as he walked past the deputy.

"Now, Deputy Bowbridge, I'm sure you were just kidding when you told my brother you weren't going to write this up," AJ said with a smirk, just waiting for the deputy to admit it.

"Well, yes, that is what I told him. There's no sign of

forced entry, and the rat poison could have ended up in the dog food by accident," he said with a smile. He obviously thought AJ was just another nobody.

"Okay then. Do you have a card? I want to make sure I give my attorney the correct information. Did I mention that my attorney is Rem Bronson?" AJ smiled knowing even this hick deputy would know the name he just dropped.

"No way is he your lawyer. He only represents clients with a lot of money," the deputy replied. Clearly, he thought AJ was just trying to scare him.

AJ selected a number on his cell phone, putting in on speaker as it rang.

"Bronson and Associates. How can I help you?" the receptionist answered.

"Hi, Bev. It's AJ Monroe. Is Rem available for a few minutes?" AJ smirked enjoying the look of disbelief on the deputy's face.

Rina looked at AJ, wonder on her face that he knew one of the most sought-after criminal defense attorneys in the country.

Jessie walked up looking much calmer than before. "What's going on?" he asked as AJ held up his hand for quiet.

"Rem Bronson here."

"Rem, it's AJ. How's it going?"

Jessie looked at the deputy and smiled a Cheshire cat smile. Rem was an old friend of AJ and Jessie's. They grew up next door to him. The three of them were insepa-rable until Rem left for college.

"Things are good here. Busy, as I'm sure you know. What's up?"

"I've got you on speaker. Jessie and I are having a little difference of opinion with a deputy here in Woodview, and we thought you could clear it up for us," AJ said as he watched the deputy start to sweat.

Jessie looked at AJ and spoke up at AJ's nod. "Hey, Rem. Jessie here. The deputy seems to think that" He stopped when the deputy held up his hand.

"I guess I was mistaken," the deputy mumbled. "I'll get the report filed right away. I'm sorry for the misunderstanding." He turned around and pulled out his notebook and started asking Rina and Jessie questions.

AJ took the phone off of speaker mode as he walked outside to talk to Rem. "Thanks, man. I knew he would freak out when I started talking to you. You should have seen the look on his face, like he had a mouthful of shit but didn't dare spit it out." He laughed along with Rem.

"Glad I could help. You ready for our camping trip?" Rem asked. "Sounds like you and Jessie are getting things back to normal between you."

"Yeah, it's been difficult, but we're working through it. We'll see you next month, man."

AJ returned to the shelter as the deputy was walking out. Still sweating and looking worried, the deputy got in his car and took off, his tires spitting gravel.

AJ watched Jessie wrap Rina in a hug. Jealousy blossomed in his chest as he stomped out the door to give them some privacy. He sat on the back bumper of Jessie's truck and ran his hands through his hair, feeling like an intruder in Jessie and Rina's relationship. After putting on his glasses, he used his phone to search for local alarm companies. He looked up when he heard the door close.

He watched Jessie stroll toward him. "Great idea, Bobo. Don't know why I didn't think of it."

"You were too pissed off to be thinking clearly. You know you have issues with that," AJ replied, thankful he was able to diffuse the situation.

Bailing Jessie out of jail was not his favorite thing to do.

He showed Jessie his phone. "I've found some local alarm companies. I'll call and see who can get out here today. We can't wait for estimates; I'm worried that if we wait, something worse will happen."

"I agree. I'll pay whatever it costs. I just want Rina to be safe. We should have them wire the house, too. I think someone should stay in Rina's house, but I don't feel it's safe for Rina. Would you do it, Bobo?"

"Sure. Do you think Rina will agree? We'll have to pay to have her electricity turned back on, and she won't like being even more in our debt," AJ said, grateful that Jessie would be the one to tell her. "She seems to have a real problem with accepting help."

"Yeah, she does, but I can't get her to talk about it," Jessie said.

"I'll get the electricity situation straightened out tomorrow along with any of her other bills that are past due," AJ remarked. "She can pay me back later. You know it won't even make a dent in my savings."

AJ walked away, dialing his cell phone to call the first alarm company on the list.

Jessie watched him walk away, knowing he needed to tell him the truth about his relationship with Rina soon. The worry for Rina on AJ's face convinced him that AJ should know the truth.

He turned and walked into the shelter, trying to decide how to tell Rina that AJ would be staying in her house for the time being, at least until they knew who was trying to shut down the shelter.

Chapter Ten

THE NEXT MORNING, AJ sat at the top of the porch stairs and stared over at the barn while he waited for the electric company to come out and turn Rina's power back on. He looked hopefully when he heard a vehicle coming up the drive.

Jessie pulled up to the house and put the shifter into park. He walked up the steps and sat next to AJ. "Hey, Bobo. I've got something I need to talk to you about."

"I'm just waiting on the electric company. I've got all the time in the world," AJ replied.

"Well, it's about me and Rina," Jessie started, pausing as if to get his thoughts in order. "It's about our relationship."

"If you want my opinion of Rina, I think she's great." He stood and walked over to the porch railing, staring out toward the horizon. "I wish you two the best of luck, but to be brutally honest"

"Let me stop you right there," Jessie interjected. "I let you think something about us that isn't true."

AJ turned and looked at Jessie, his eyes blazing. "You better not tell me that you're just using her." He turned his back to Jessie, trying to get his emotions under control.

"Bobo, look at me." Jessie sighed hoping that AJ wouldn't punch him. "Rina is not my girlfriend."

"What? So, you're telling me you two are not together?" AJ asked incredulously. "You're just friends?"

"Yes, that's what I'm saying. I guess I just wanted you to sweat a little, so I let you continue to think she was my girlfriend," Jessie answered. "Purely platonic. But I can tell you're interested."

"Thanks for telling me, Jess," AJ said with a smile, already thinking of ways to let Rina know how he felt. His mood plummeted when he remembered what she said that day on the porch when he found her: "Love you, Jessie". Obviously Jessie had no idea how she really felt about him. He thought they were just friends.

A van from the electric company pulled up giving AJ something to deal with other than trying to figure out how to tell Jessie that Rina loved him. After the electric was turned back on, Jessie checked out Rina's house and verified there were no problems with the power before he let the technician leave. As he strolled through the house, he noticed some things that needed work: leaky faucets, peeling wallpaper, and faded paint. After locking up, he drove toward Jessie's to pick up his clothes.

An hour later, he was back at Rina's with Gunner and

his suitcase. He wondered if Jessie had told her about him paying her bills and staying in her house. As he unpacked his suitcase in what looked like a guest room, he heard a vehicle pull up and looked out the window. At this rate, he'd never get the van running.

Rina strolled in noticing the power was back on. "I know you're here, AJ. Jessie told me where to find you." She stood in the living room and waited for AJ to come to her. "You paid the electric bill?" Her face was turning red in anger. "Who the hell told you to do that?"

"Now listen, Rina. Jessie and I thought it would be better to have someone staying in your house to keep an eye on the shelter," AJ said, trying to calm her with logic.

"I did not give either one of you permission to pay my bills!" she yelled. "I will not rely on someone else to take care of me. I can pay my own way!" She stomped across the floor until she stood face to face with him. "I got my job back at the diner. I will have the money to pay you back next week."

She walked over to the couch and pulled up the cushion, obviously looking for the bills she had shoved under there. "Don't tell me. You paid all of them, didn't you?" she asked softly, sounding much calmer.

"Well, yeah, I did," AJ replied, glad she was speaking more calmly. "You can pay me back when you get the money. No rush."

"That is not the point!" she screeched. "I didn't ask you to do that!" She turned and stomped out the door, calling Petey to follow her.

"Great. Now she's pissed at both of us," AJ said to himself. He watched out the window as she walked around the shelter, taking the path to Jessie's. "Why does she react that way toward someone trying to help her?" He called Jessie and let him know Rina was on her way and she was pissed.

Chapter Eleven

TWO DAYS WENT by with no incidents at the shelter. The alarm system and AJ's presence seemed to have been effective at stopping the break-ins. Rina's temper had not cooled; she ignored both Jessie and AJ unless it was absolutely necessary to interact with them. AJ had fixed the van's engine, but there was no way he was going to tell her how much he spent on parts. He had turned his attention to Rina's house and had fixed the leaky faucets and was now patching drywall and removing wallpaper. He knew it would piss Rina off, but he just couldn't help himself. Besides, working on his book only took up so much time each day.

Tired of working indoors, he let the sun and blue sky entice him outside. It was a perfect day to spend outdoors. A walk to Jessie's sounded like just the thing to clear his mind, and he could check if his brother had any sandpaper. The shelter was quiet. Rina had left for her lunch shift at the diner about fifteen minutes prior, so he checked that all the doors were locked before walking down the path, enjoying the solitude and the warm weather. When he arrived at Jessie's, he dug around in the garage for sandpaper with no luck. Oh well, it was a beautiful day for a walk. The weather made him wish he had his 'Cuda. It was the perfect time of year for a convertible.

He almost had Rina's house in his sight when he heard the dogs barking. He took off running. As he trotted up the hill from behind the shelter, he spied a car speeding down the driveway and turning left onto the road. He cursed the sweat running in his eyes as he tried to read the license plate. He spotted the graffiti when he turned to walk back to the shelter and check on the dogs. Someone had painted sexually explicit graffiti all over the barn.

"Damn. How did they know there wasn't anyone around? Are they watching the place?"

The sound of a vehicle speeding up the drive put his senses on high alert. He moved out of sight behind the barn so the driver wouldn't see him. He stepped back out from the building when he saw it was his brother.

Jessie leaped out of his truck and slammed the door. "When did this happen?" he asked, pointing at the graffiti. "I thought you were here to prevent things like this from happening."

"I walked over to your place to look for some sandpaper. I needed a break from indoor work." He turned at the sound of another vehicle driving up, grimacing at the sight of the van. "Rina is not going to be happy about this."

Rina slid out of the van. "Really? You've got to be kidding me." She started to pace, "I'm about ready to give up," she mumbled, her shoulders slumping. "I don't know how much more of this I can take."

She unlocked the door and walked into the barn, trying to soothe the dogs who were still riled up and barking like crazy. "All right, guys. That'll do! Settle down!"

Jessie looked at AJ. "I'll head to town and get some paint and primer. We can't leave the graffiti. The whole town would be scandalized, and Rina has enough problems already." He walked to his truck, shaking his head at the graffiti. "Why would someone do this to Rina?"

"You ready to tell me what's going on here?" AJ asked Rina, wanting to grab her and kiss her until she told him the truth. "This has been going on for a while hasn't it?"

Rina sighed. "It's nothing. I can handle it," she said as she turned away from AJ to walk into the barn.

AJ grabbed her arm, pulling her around to face him. "What is the big secret?" he asked, leading her toward the house instead. He dragged her up the porch steps and sat her in one of the rockers. "Now, tell me what's going on. Whoever this is has tried to poison the dogs. I want to help you deal with this, but I need to know the whole story." The thought that they might go after her next scared him more than he wanted to admit.

Rina looked down at her hands. "It's not your fight. I can deal with it on my own."

"What if they go after you instead of the dogs next

time? How are you going to protect yourself?" He turned away from her and stared across the lawn toward the road, not wanting her to see the worry in his eyes. "I don't want anyone to hurt you…" He couldn't finish his thought, couldn't tell her it would tear him up if she were hurt.

He jumped when he felt Rina's hand come around his waist from behind. She laid her head on his back. "You act all worried about me, but you flinch when I touch you. Why?"

"This isn't about me. It's about you and these people who are after you." He stepped out of her embrace. "Dammit. How can I help if you won't talk to me?" He stood at the door and faced her. "When you're ready to talk, let me know," he said just before he let the screen door slam.

Rina sat back down on the rocker, fighting back the tears. "I think you're wrong, Mama. AJ and Jessie aren't like Daddy. They won't leave me with nothing to find my own way," she said to herself.

Halfway to town, Jessie pulled up in front of a car parked on the other side of the road, noticing the flat tire. Shutting off his truck, he looked for the driver of the car. He watched a curvy blonde slam the trunk lid shut, obviously upset. "Dammit! How in the hell am I supposed to change a tire with no jack?" she yelled, unaware Jessie was there to hear. "Why me?" she implored, looking up as if God would answer from the sky.

Jessie ambled toward the blonde. "Hey there. Need some help?" He had to remind himself to breathe when he noticed her brown eyes that seemed to be spitting fire. He looked her up and down, wondering where such a beauty came from.

"My eyes are up here, soldier," she said with a smirk when she noticed where Jessie's gaze seemed to have stopped. "I am more than just my boobs."

Jessie looked up. "Uh, sorry. Can I help you with that flat tire?" he asked, trying to keep his thoughts on the tire and off of her. Her curves and cleavage seemed to have vapor locked his brain. Then it sunk in that she had called him soldier. "How did you know I was military?"

"You just have that look about you. What branch?" she asked, her gaze locked with his as she waited for him to answer.

"Marines."

"Thank you for your service. Now, my jack seems to be missing. Do you have one I can use?"

"I've got one in my truck. Why don't you find some shade, and I'll get that tire changed for you," he said, looking her up and down again. He gave himself a mental head slap to quit ogling her or she was going to think he was a total perv.

She stepped around to the side of the car, and he had to remind himself to quit staring. The cutoff shorts she was wearing showed off the length of her legs, and he had to quickly turn and head to his truck for the jack before she saw the obvious effect she was having on him. He acted as if he were digging around in his truck to try and get rid of the wood he was sporting. His jeans weren't loose enough to hide it.

After getting his libido under control, he grabbed the

jack and the lug wrench and walked back to her car. He could feel her watching as he bent over to place the jack under the axle. He flexed his muscles as he loosened the lug nuts. Might as well give her a show.

"So, what brings you to Indiana?" he asked, turning to look at her when she didn't answer right away.

She blushed at being caught staring at him as he worked. "Woodview is my hometown."

He grinned as he heaved the spare tire out, giving his muscles a little extra flex now that he knew she was watching. "Are you back to stay?" he asked, moving the tire into position and tightened the lug nuts, hoping she would say yes.

"Yeah."

He pulled a rag out of his pocket and wiped off his hands, giving her time to elaborate. He looked up and noticed the resignation in her eyes before she could hide it. He wondered what had driven her back to her hometown where she obviously didn't want to be.

"You're all set," he said as he turned and walked back toward his truck, hoping she would stop him. He looked back when he heard her car door close and her car start. She pulled away without even a glance back at him. He settled into his truck, wondering why she didn't seem to be happy to be home. He resumed his drive into town to get the primer and paint.

Dori pulled into Rina's driveway, lost in thought about her encounter with the hot marine. She was attracted to him, but it was too soon. It had only been a couple of days since she broke up with Ty. She shuddered at the memory of his hands on her the last time they fought and rubbed the bruise on the inside of her wrist. Luckily, a friend of his had stopped by, and she had been able to slip away. Looking up, she spied the graffiti on the barn. "What the hell?" she said, slamming the car door. "Rina?" she yelled, hoping her friend was okay.

Rina walked out of the barn with Petey close on her heels. He ran to Dori, jumping up until she reached down and gave him some scratches.

"Hi, Petey! How you doing?" she asked, looking up when she heard Rina approaching. She stood and gave Rina a hug, frowning at how thin she seemed. "Hey, girl. Surprise!"

"What are you doing here?" Rina asked. "Did Ty come with you?"

"No. I left him. I didn't know where else to go, so I hopped in the car and headed here."

Dori looked up when she heard the screen door, ready to run if Ty had made it here before her. "How did you get here before me?" she asked AJ. "You were headed the other direction." She looked at him closer and blushed. "Wait. You're not him."

"Him who?" AJ asked with a grin.

"Someone who looks an awful lot like you stopped and changed my flat tire for me."

"That was my brother, Jessie. I'm impressed you can tell us apart. Most people can't."

Rina spoke up. "This is my friend Dori. Dori, this is

AJ. His brother, Jessie, lives over in the Winter's place." Jealousy blossomed in her chest at the way AJ seemed to be looking at Dori. "Jessie and AJ have been helping me out with the shelter." She turned her attention to AJ. "Dori and I went to high school together. She ran off with her boyfriend after graduation."

Dori took advantage of the lull in the conversation. "I've been on the road for hours and really need to use the restroom. I'll be right back," she said as she ran into the house.

Rina looked at AJ. "Don't say anything to her about what's going on. I don't want to drag her into my mess. Please."

"Okay."

Rina stared at him with longing as he turned and sauntered over to the trailer hooked up to the SUV and lifted up a sheet of drywall. Her mouth went dry as she watched his muscles bulge and bunch from his efforts. Why couldn't she get him to notice her interest?

Dropping down onto the porch steps, she let her tears run silently down her face. She stood when Jessie drove up with the painting supplies and quickly wiped away the evidence of her tears, not wanting Jessie to know she'd been crying.

"Where's AJ?" he asked. "You've been crying. What did he do? Do you want me to go beat him up for you?" It upset him to see her cry, especially over his thick-headed brother.

She smiled at his cavalier words. "It's nothing like

that. I just gave AJ the perfect opportunity to kiss me, and he walked away again. I don't understand your brother at all." She grabbed a couple of paint cans and swung them out of the back of the truck. "Let's get started with the paint. I really don't want to look at the graffiti any longer."

"Go ahead and get started. I need to talk to AJ for a minute." He walked up the porch steps. "Sounds like I need to pound some sense into him," he muttered to himself as he reached for the screen door. "AJ? Where the hell are you?"

A piece of sandpaper in his hand, AJ stomped out of the other room, pulling down his dust mask. "What? I'm trying to get the drywall done in here," he growled.

"What's got your panties in a twist?" Jessie asked. "I want to talk to you about Rina." He sat on the sheet-covered sofa and threw his keys on the end table. "I thought I told you that Rina and I are not together. She told me she's been trying to let you know she's interested, but you keep ignoring her."

"Yes, you did tell me. But did you tell her?" he inquired.

"Why do you keep asking me that? I told you I think of her as a little sister."

AJ paced the length of the room before turning back.

"Would you just tell me why you're making such a big deal about it?"

"I'll tell you why," AJ said through gritted teeth. "Because she loves you. There, I said it. You happy now?"

he snarled. "I'm sure she's only acting interested in me to make you jealous or something."

AJ walked over to the window and stared out at Rina spreading primer over the graffiti on the barn. "She said she loves you. That first day, she looked up at me and said 'Love you, Jessie'."

"She's said that to me, too, but she added that she loves me like a brother." Jessie still didn't understand why this was bothering AJ so much. The only time they had an issue with a girl was the whole Sasha situation. "You know I don't love her as anything other than a friend. Why is this bugging you?"

AJ looked over at Jessie. "Do you realize how many girls propositioned me in high school? There were a lot, and they all wanted you and settled for me, the 'not as cool' brother. They all eventually admitted they were only with me to get closer to you or that they were pretending I was you." AJ grabbed Jessie's keys off the end table and strode out the door without a word. He jumped in Jessie's truck and took off.

Jessie ran his hands through his hair, wondering why his brother had never disclosed that bit of information to him before. He turned to walk out the door and noticed Dori peeking out of the bathroom, looking to see if the coast was clear.

"Hey, beauty. What are you doing here?"

Startled by his voice, she put her arms up over her head to protect her face. "Geez, you scared me."

Dismayed by her reaction, he followed her into the kitchen and watched as she pulled a bottle of water out of the fridge. She looked at him and waved the water bottle in her hand. Grabbing one for him at his nod, she handed it to him before walking out to the front porch.

"Why did you react like you were expecting me to hit you," he asked, wanting to punch someone for making her afraid. He remembered her saying she was moving back, but she only had one suitcase in the car with her. "Who are you running from?"

"My ex-boyfriend," she said with a frown. "I don't know why I came here. This is the first place he'll look for me." She wrapped her arms around herself as if to hold herself together. "Coming here was a stupid idea." She sobbed.

He reached out and put his hand on her shoulder to show he understood what it was like to run from your demons, whether they're memories or people. Turning to face him, she wrapped her arms around him and let her tears flow.

"Well, hell," he murmured, holding her closely. "It's okay, beauty. I won't let anything happen to you." He didn't even know her name, but he would lay down his life for her without hesitating. The thought of someone putting their hands on her made him clench his hands into fists in preparation for beating someone bloody.

Her sobs tapered off, and her breathing evened out. She lifted her head and looked at him, brushing at the wet spots on his shirt from her tears. "Thanks," she said. "I'm sorry about your shirt." A smile pulled at her tear-stained lips. "I do have a name, you know."

"You do?" He smirked. "I haven't heard it yet."

"You must think I'm a complete ditz." She brushed the tears off of her face. "My name is Dori Graham."

He gently wiped away a tear she missed from under her eye. "I don't think that, Dori. You just had more important things on your mind," he replied before kissing her on the forehead. With a grimace, he limped down the steps, his knee sending waves of pain up his leg.

"Why are you limping?"

"That's a story for another time. Let's just say it's the reason I'm not a marine anymore and leave it at that for now." He didn't like talking about his time in Afghanistan where he watched good men die from horrible wounds. "Rina is probably wondering where you are by now." He held his hand out to help her navigate the stairs and gave her a hug before walking off toward the barn where the paint was waiting for him.

AJ drove toward town, not headed anywhere in particular. He pulled into the parking lot of a park, deciding the mostly deserted lot would do as a place for him to think. Shutting off the engine, he let his thoughts have free reign. The dog tags hanging from the mirror reminded him he loved his brother even while he hated how girls treated him as if he were just a stand-in for the popular Monroe brother. Jessie was the one who had played basketball and dated the cheerleaders. Even Sasha had been that 'type': blonde and cute and always upbeat.

I'm not him, he thought. *I was the nerdy one always with my nose in a book or a video game.* It dawned on him he needed to feel resentment toward the girls who treated him that way, not Jessie. His twin didn't have any control over what those girls did; he hadn't even known it was happening. Realizing he let the past color his actions in the present, he wanted to apologize to his brother and to Rina. He composed his apologies in his head and hoped Rina would give him another chance.

Chapter Twelve

PARKING IN FRONT of the barn, AJ listened to Rina and Jessie bantering back and forth. He should have noticed it before, but he had been too focused on the past to see what was right in front of him. They bickered back and forth like siblings, not like a couple in love. He smiled, thoughts of getting his lips on Rina's again consuming his mind. He watched Dori rolling paint like a pro and stealing glances at Jessie when he wasn't looking.

Slamming the truck door, AJ advanced toward her. Rina turned and stared at him with fire in her eyes, fire for him, not Jessie. He took the roller out of her hand and dropped it into the paint tray. Grabbing her hand, he pulled her around to the back of the barn.

Rina tried to pull her arm out of his grasp. "AJ, what are you do"

He covered her lips with his and poured all his unresolved feelings for her into the kiss.

She melted against him as his hands ran through her hair before moving down to her butt, lifting her up so she was nestled against him. Her right leg wrapped around him, pulling him even closer as his tongue explored her mouth. Breathing heavily, he broke away and leaned his forehead against hers.

"I need to apologize for the way I've been treating you. There were some old hurts getting in the way of how I feel for you," he said. He stared into her eyes, looking for anger or resentment but seeing only compassion and longing. "How about we start over? Hi, I'm AJ." He stuck his hand out and grinned. "And you are?"

"I'm Rina. Very nice to meet you, handsome," she replied with a wicked gleam in her eyes. "Now that we've been properly introduced…" She wrapped her arms around his neck and pulled his head down and kissed him, long and slow and deep.

Jessie ran a shaky hand through his hair when she pulled back. "Wow." He sighed as he worked to get himself under control. She lowered her eyes shyly when he ran his thumb over her bottom lip as if she were afraid of what she'd see in his eyes. "Rina"

"I know. That was way too intense, and we need to go slower," she said. "I better get back to painting." She turned and stepped back around the barn, stopping just before turning that last corner to compose herself and battle with her tears. "God, I'm an idiot."

"No, you're not, Rina. You didn't let me finish before you totally went off in the wrong direction." He wiped a tear off her face. "You've got me so tied up in knots I can't even think straight." He reached out and pulled her into him, holding her closely. "I don't want to slow anything down, but any more kisses like that and I may spontaneously combust," he said with a laugh. "You affect me like no other woman ever has. Now, go paint, and we'll talk more about all of this later." He gave her a short, sweet kiss and then shoved her toward the front of the barn. He leaned against the barn and willed his heart to beat normally again as he watched her disappear around the corner. Just being near her sent his heart rate soaring.

Rounding the corner of the barn, he watched Rina stumble her way over to the paint roller she had been using before he interrupted. She picked up the roller and stood there staring at it.

"Rina? You trying to paint the wall telepathically?" Jessie asked with a grin. "Looks like my brother does know what to do with a woman," he said to Dori with a laugh. He continued to paint, whistling happily. When he spied AJ looking just as shell-shocked as Rina, he laughed again, glad he wasn't the one walking around like a zombie. "Better you than me, Bro," he muttered to himself as he rolled more paint onto the wall in front of him.

AJ sauntered back to the house to continue his work on the drywall, unable to believe that just a couple of hours ago he had been ready to punch his brother out of jealousy. Now, he knew the truth. She wanted him, nerdy AJ, instead of Jessie the jock. He shook his head trying to get rid of the old stereotypes as he pulled the dust mask down and started sanding.

After an hour of sanding without a break, the drywall dust irritated his lungs, making him cough and bringing on the tight feeling of an asthma attack. A blast from his inhaler brought back memories of the daily struggle he had with his asthma while he was growing up, making him grateful he only had to use it occasionally instead of daily. Not wanting to risk a full-blown attack, he would have to get Jessie to finish the sanding. As his breathing eased, all he could think about was kissing Rina again, causing him to breathe heavier in a different way. Those lips and that body had him tied up in knots.

Unable to still his thoughts, he turned on his phone and sent her a text: *Want 2 go out to dinner tonight?*

Absently brushing her hair, Rina tried to push thoughts of AJ away so she could concentrate on planning what to cook for dinner. Frustrated at her lack of focus, she grabbed her phone when she heard the text notification, glad for any distraction to get her mind off of the kiss. She smiled and replied, *Yes!!*

He texted back, *Pick u up at 6.*

"That was AJ, wasn't it?" Dori asked, noticing the silly grin spread across Rina's face from her spot on the bed.

"Yeah, we're going out to dinner. Oh God. What am I going to wear?" Frantic, she rummaged through the clothes in the closet, grimacing at the lack of choices. "I'm going to have to go home and get something. I don't have anything here that will work." She picked up her purse and pulled Dori with her toward the door. "Come on. You've got to help me find something."

Dori stopped. "Slow down. Your closet isn't going anywhere. I just need to grab my phone."

Rina stared at her phone as she waited for her friend, thinking about finally being alone with AJ.

She jumped when Jessie knocked on the doorframe.

"What do you want for dinner tonight? I could go pick up Chinese."

"None for me." She grinned. "I have a date. See ya later, Jessie!" she yelled over her shoulder as she sprinted out of the house with Dori right behind her.

Dori turned and yelled back to Jessie. "Chinese sounds great! I'll text you…" Rina pulled her out the door to the sound of Jessie's laughter.

Rina couldn't believe it when she walked into the dining room in her house. Even without paint, the room looked so much better. She ran her hands along the drywall, wondering how she was going to pay AJ back for all his hard work. The wall was smooth, no signs of the gouges and holes from when someone broke in and punched holes in her walls.

"What do you think?"

She jumped and turned to find AJ leaning in the doorway.

"Geez. I think you scared ten years off my life." She laughed as she put her arms around him and hugged him, planting a quick kiss on his lips. "It looks wonderful," she exclaimed as she placed her hand on his cheek, noticing how smooth it felt. Deciding it was not the time to talk about paying him back, she simply smiled and said, "Thank you."

"You're welcome, Rina. I'm glad to do it. Plus, it gives me plenty of time to think about my book." He brushed a kiss across her lips. "I'm just curious how you ended up with so many holes in the wall."

She turned away, not wanting to explain about the break-in. "Well, I need to get ready for our date. Can you give me about forty minutes?" She looked around realizing Dori was nowhere in sight. "Where's Dori?"

"I think she snuck upstairs. I need to go talk to Jessie, but I'll be back. Don't forget to set the alarm when I leave." He backed away from her as if he didn't want to let her out of his sight.

She set the alarm and skipped up the stairs to see what Dori found in her closet that would be date-appropriate. The sundress and sandals Dori had picked out were perfect for the balmy late summer weather. The water rained down on her while standing in the shower debating when and how to tell AJ everything about her situation, including how she grew up. But not tonight. Tonight they would be on a date, so no secret revealing allowed. She'd tell him everything the next day.

Talking and giggling with Dori as she prepared for her date reminded her of high school when they would take hours getting ready for a dance or a date. Dori picked out earrings as Rina finished up her makeup. After attaching the earrings, she stepped over to the full-length mirror.

"I feel like a princess. It's been so long since I dressed

up or went out with a guy." She glanced over at the night-stand when one of their phones chirped.

Dori picked up her phone. "It was mine. Jessie wants to know what I want from Ming's." She typed in her order and hit send as Rina's phone chirped. She carried it over to Rina. "Is AJ ready to go? You are so lucky. You should see the way he looks at you when he thinks no one is looking." She fanned herself. "Those looks should be sending you up in flames!"

Rina smiled. "Yeah, he is pretty great."

They heard the sound of a vehicle coming up the drive, and Rina peeked out the window. "That's him. I'll see you later at Jessie's." She walked to the stairs, turning for one last comment to her friend. "Don't forget to set the alarm when you leave."

AJ looked up when he heard Rina at the top of the stairs. The sight of her in a dress made him feel as stupid and tongue-tied as a teenager on his first date. "God, how did I get so lucky?" he whispered, trying to swallow the lump in his throat. "Hey," he said, his voice cracking. He cleared his throat and tried again. "Hey, Rina. You ready?" He hoped she was because if she looked any better, he wouldn't be able to string two words together coherently.

She walked down the stairs, limping slightly. His eyes traveled down her bare legs to her heeled sandals, and his mouth went dry. Rina stepped off the last stair into AJ's arms.

"Have fun!" Dori yelled.

Nervous about their date, Rina stared out the window as AJ drove them into town.

AJ brushed her hair off her shoulder. "Hey, why so quiet?"

"You make me nervous."

"I make you nervous?" He cleared his throat. "I'm just a teacher, nothing special."

"But that's not all. You're a published author. I'm just a small town girl. What can you possibly see in me?"

He looked at her, dumbfounded. "What do I see in you? I see a beautiful woman who cares about abandoned animals the way some people care about their family."

She blushed and looked down at her hands, shoving her mother's voice into a box in her mind and locking it. "But you're a teacher responsible for shaping young minds along with writing a book that other people want to read."

"What you do for those dogs is more important than any story I may write." He took her hand and held it in his, interlacing their fingers before bringing it up to his mouth and kissing the back of it. "You're beautiful and caring. What's not to love?"

She gazed out the windshield at the fields flying by, her mind whirling with thoughts of AJ and her growing feelings for him.

When they arrived at the restaurant, he coughed again, and his breathing became labored and wheezy.

"AJ? You okay?"

He nodded as he pulled an inhaler out of his pocket and used it.

Rina rubbed his back as his breathing eased, her eyes showing her concern.

"Sorry about that." He took another dose from the inhaler. "I have asthma."

"It was scary watching you struggle to breathe, but it's nothing to be ashamed of. Do you have attacks often? Oh God. It was my perfume, wasn't it?"

"Hey, it wasn't your perfume. I was sanding drywall in the dining room today, and that aggravated it. Now, let's get in there and get our table. I'm starving. Let's talk about this later."

She wondered why he seemed to want to downplay the attack. With his hand at her back, he escorted her into the steakhouse.

Seated in a corner booth, they perused the menu and decided on their choices for dinner. Once their drinks were delivered, he pulled her closer to him and draped his arm over her shoulders.

"I'm sorry you had to witness the asthma attack. I hate when they happen in public." He sipped his tea and cleared his throat. "I've had asthma as long as I can remember. I spent a lot of time in hospitals when I was a kid until it was under control. Now, I only have attacks when I'm overstressed or I do something stupid like sand drywall all day."

She looked up at him, feeling guilty. "No more drywall sanding for you. I'm having a talk with your brother tomorrow."

They were interrupted by the waitress carrying out their meals. Once she set the plates on the table, she asked, "Anything else?" She smiled and leaned over to adjust the plate placement, the neckline of her blouse at his eye level, her cleavage on display.

"No, thank you," Rina replied. "That will be all."

The waitress turned her attention to Rina, her smile morphing into a scowl, and walked away.

"What was that about?" he asked as he buttered his roll.

"She was totally flirting with you. You are obviously here on a date, and she was trying to get you to notice her."

"I don't think so. Why would she flirt with me?"

"Seriously? Have you looked in the mirror lately?"

"I'm used to being the not as popular twin. Growing up, Jessie was the popular one, playing sports and getting the cheerleaders to go out with him. Girls only paid attention to me to get closer to my brother."

"That may have been true then but not anymore." She blushed as she continued. "You're good looking, you have a steady job, and you're a published author." *And,* she added silently, *you are so hot when you're wearing your glasses.*

Smiling at her compliment, he turned the conversation to her. "Enough about me. What about you? Did you grow up in Woodview?"

She sipped at her wine, trying to formulate an answer that would satisfy him without revealing anything about her current situation.

"Hang on. My phone just buzzed. Let me turn it to silent." Noticing he had a text from his brother, he opened it. "We need to go. Jessie and Dori are at the hospital."

"What happened?" She jumped up and grabbed her purse, afraid he would tell her that Dori had been hurt by her ex.

"I don't know," he said as he dialed his phone.

The waitress hurried over at his wave. "Is everything okay? Was there a problem with your food?"

He held up his hand and started talking into his phone.

Rina answered for him. "The food was fine. We have an emergency and have to leave. Can you please get our bill?"

"Sure thing." She hurried off and returned with the bill in her hand.

Once they had paid the bill, they hurried out to the truck. AJ stomped on the gas and drove toward the hospital.

"You're scaring me. It's Dori, isn't it?"

"Yes, it is. She's fine – nothing a few stitches can't fix."

"Then what's the hurry?"

He pulled into the hospital parking lot and parked in the first open space. "I'll explain once I talk to Jessie."

Jessie and the doctor walked out the door to find AJ and Rina waiting anxiously.

"Is she okay?" Rina asked. She looked like she would shatter into a million pieces any minute. AJ's cryptic answers had her worried about her friend.

"Hey. She's okay. Just a few stitches, and she'll be as good as new," Jessie told her as he pulled her into a hug.

He set her away from him, placing his hands on her shoulders. "Her attacker thought she was you. I know you're not telling us everything about the problems you've been having with break-ins at the shelter and why you can't access your money. We will talk about this tomorrow, and you will tell us the truth. It's affecting other people now." He tried to keep the anger out of his voice, but finding Dori tied up and bleeding had shaken him up more than he wanted to admit.

"This is all my fault." Rina tried to hold back the tears. "I didn't think anyone else would get hurt."

AJ pulled her out of Jessie's arms, frowning at her tears. "We'll make sure everyone is safe, Rina. Everything will be okay. I promise." He looked over at Jessie. "You make sure the girls are safe tonight. I'll make sure the dogs are okay. Between the two of us, we should be able to keep an eye on everything."

Jessie walked back into the treatment room, followed by AJ and Rina.

Rina rushed over to Dori. "I'm so sorry! This is all my fault."

"No, it's not. I forgot to set the alarm after you left. It was like an open invitation for the guy to just come on in. He probably wouldn't have hurt me if I hadn't tried to get away." She reached up and felt the dried blood caked in her hair. "Ugh! Can you help me wash my hair tonight? This is gross."

"Sure, I'll get you fixed up." Rina looked up when the nurse walked in with Dori's discharge paperwork. "Do you want me to call your dad?" she asked.

"No!" Dori replied heatedly. "I don't want to talk to him. Don't you call him" She stopped when she realized the nurse was staring at her.

"Here's your discharge paperwork and wound care instructions."

Two hours later, the girls were parked on the couch, flipping through channels to find something they wanted to watch. Jessie strolled over with a bowl of popcorn and a glass of wine, handing both to Rina.

Dori looked up at him. "Hey, where's mine?"

"No alcohol for you tonight. Ladies on pain meds don't get to drink," he said with a grin as AJ walked in and handed her a soda. "You'll just have to deal with it. I'll take you out for drinks tomorrow night."

"You are no fun," she said continuing the banter. "I guess if you're going to be the alcohol police, I'll have to be a good girl tonight. Drinks tomorrow night sounds great."

They settled on a chick flick, eliciting groans from both AJ and Jessie. Jessie sat next to Dori with his arm around her. About halfway through the movie, Jessie noticed that both Rina and Dori had fallen asleep. AJ stood, moving slowly to avoid waking Rina. He picked her up and carried her into the guest bedroom, kissing her and telling her goodnight when she opened her eyes and looked at him sleepily. He kissed her again, regretting that he had to leave to go check on the dogs and stay alone in her empty house as a deterrent to whomever is causing all the problems with the shelter.

AJ walked out of the bedroom. "I guess I better get

going and check on the dogs. I think we should have someone at Rina's twenty-four seven after what happened today."

Jessie nodded. "I agree. I have to go back to work next week. I hope we can get this cleared up by then."

AJ called Gunner and walked to the door. "I'll let you know if anything happens. Be safe, Bro."

"You, too."

Chapter Thirteen

THE NEXT MORNING, Jessie drove Rina and Dori over to Rina's to help with the dogs. After he unlocked the door and checked all the rooms, Jessie let the girls start cleaning kennels and tend to other odds and ends around the shelter. He walked toward the house to talk to AJ, stopping when Cam pulled in and parked next to his truck.

"Morning, Cam. Glad you could make it. Sorry I had to call you so early on your day off, but we need your help. AJ is in the house. Let's go talk there."

They walked into the house, finding AJ patching drywall in the kitchen.

"You're here early," AJ remarked to Cam.

"Had a meeting at the station this morning. Is there coffee?"

"I think there's still some in the pot. Let's go sit on the back deck so we can keep an eye on the shelter. I don't like having Rina out of my sight for very long."

After they all filled mugs with coffee, Jessie grabbed a

notebook and followed the others out to the deck and sat around the table.

AJ cleared his throat. "So, Cam, last night you said you might have an idea who is behind the break-ins and money problems Rina has been having. I think it's more involved than Rina has been letting on," he said with a glare at his brother. "I can't believe you didn't notice anything, Jess. This has to have been going on for a while now. Dori said the guy said something about a last warning, so obviously Rina has been having problems for some time."

They all looked up when they saw Rina and Dori walk out of the barn and head toward the deck.

"You want some coffee?" Jessie asked as the girls pulled chairs over to the table.

"We're good. Hey, Cam," Rina said.

"Okay, Rina. I think it's time you let us in on the big secret. You need to tell us what is going on," Jessie said. He pulled the notebook closer to him and took a pen out of his pocket.

Rina looked over at him. "I don't know where to start. It's been going on for so long."

AJ grabbed her hand, lacing their fingers and pulling her hand up to his mouth for a kiss.

Rina took a deep breath and started to explain. "It started when I inherited the farm from my grandfather. After the deed was transferred to my name and I got the paperwork submitted for the permits to open the shelter, I was visited by the town bad boys."

Cam frowned and held up his hand for Rina to stop.

"Rina, it started a long time before that. It's been going on for years. Anyone who owns a business in this town will tell you. Someone has a nice little protection racket going on here in Woodview. I'm sure your grandfather was paying them before he died. It's the only way a business survives in this town."

Rina looked over at Cam, eyes wide in disbelief. "It isn't just me?" She stood and paced the length of the deck. "They told me if I didn't pay, they would empty my accounts and have the permits for the shelter revoked."

AJ got up and walked over to Rina and pulled her into his arms. "You didn't pay them, did you?"

"No, of course not."

"Well, that explains a lot." He kissed Rina on the top of her head and guided her toward her chair. "When I brought her home from the hospital, I found her electricity had been disconnected and a pile of unpaid bills shoved under a couch cushion."

Rina flushed. "Because I didn't pay them, they made good on their threat. All my accounts were frozen, and I was suddenly fired from my waitressing job. When AJ found me, I don't think I'd had a decent meal for a couple of weeks. All the money I had went to dog food and supplies for the shelter." She looked down at her hands. "I was only eating once a day, and that was usually a peanut butter sandwich."

Jessie started to grind his teeth. "Why didn't you tell me or Cam? We would have at least made sure you had food. Jesus, Rina. We would have helped."

Rina turned red. "You need to understand what my life

was like before I came to live with Grandpa. My mother always relied on someone else to take care of her. She wasn't capable of looking after herself, much less her daughter."

"What do you mean?" AJ asked, almost afraid to hear the answer.

Cam stood and tried to release some of the tension. "Anyone else need some more coffee? I'll brew another pot. It sounds like this may take some time."

Rina turned in her chair and stared out over the fields behind Jessie's house, trying to quell the sick feeling in her stomach. She knew she needed to tell them her story, but it wouldn't be easy. The memories of those days made her feel cold and alone. When Cam returned with fresh coffee, she gratefully wrapped her fingers around her cup to warm them after he filled it. She stared into her cup as if the answer to life's mysteries could be found there.

AJ put his hand on her arm. "Do you want to tell all of us now? You could just tell it to one of us, you know."

She took a deep breath and straightened her shoulders. "No. It will be better if I tell all of you at once." She took a drink of her coffee. "My life was great until Daddy died when I was eight." AJ grabbed her hand, willing her to have the strength to talk about her life. "Before Daddy died, there was just enough money to keep the wolf from the door. We didn't have much, but we had each other. Then when Daddy died, my mom changed. She couldn't manage anything as simple as balancing the checkbook or paying the bills on time. Daddy was the one who took care of all that. All Mom had to do was take care of the house and take care of me and Daddy. After he died, she couldn't even handle that."

AJ squeezed her hand, lending her his strength.

"Six months after Daddy died, we lost the house. We lived in our car for a while until Mom found a boyfriend, and we moved in with him. He was the first in a long line of boyfriends. Things would be fine for a couple of months, and then it would just fall apart, and we would be back out on the streets. By the time I was ten, she had been introduced to drugs by one of her boyfriends, and any money that came in went to support her new habit. When I was twelve, she overdosed and died." She pushed away from the table, tears coursing down her cheeks as she stood with her back to everyone.

AJ went to her and pulled her into a hug, letting her cry. He rubbed his hand up and down her back, trying to soothe her grief. Cam and Jessie took Dori into the house, letting AJ and Rina have some time alone.

Cam looked at the time on his phone. "I didn't realize it was that late. I'm supposed to meet my girlfriend at the diner in twenty minutes for lunch. Let me know what you need me to do."

Dori grabbed the bread off the counter and starting pulling lunch meat out of the fridge, needing something to keep her hands and her mind busy. She had no idea what Rina had gone through before she came to live in Woodview with her grandfather. She started making sandwiches for everyone, sniffing to try and keep the tears from falling. Jessie walked up and put his hand on her shoulder and turned her around to face him. He scowled when she stiffened up at his touch.

"Come here, beauty," he said. He pulled her into his arms and tucked her head under his chin. He held her closely, wanting to get his hands on whoever made her afraid to be touched.

She looked up when they heard the door open. AJ walked in, his shoulders slumped and his eyes downcast as he pulled a bottle of water out of the fridge. Without a word, he shuffled out of the kitchen.

"You okay now, beauty?" Jessie asked.

At her nod, he let her go and followed AJ out of room.

Jessie found AJ in Rina's room sitting on the bed, his inhaler in his hand. "You okay, Bro?" He walked in and sat on the bed next to him. He could hear AJ wheezing. He looked at him. "I thought you were done with the asthma."

AJ used the inhaler again. Taking a slow, deep breath, he noticed the wheezing had subsided. "It only flares up when I let myself get too stressed. I usually only use an inhaler once every couple of weeks, but worrying about Rina has got me tied up in knots." He stood and started pacing. "I don't know how she ended up being so impor-tant to me in such a short time." He stood at the window with his hands in his pockets, staring out at the sky. "It's as if finding her out cold on your porch turned on this protective feeling. I've felt it before but never this intensely. And then she looks at me with those eyes..." He ran his hands through his hair, trying to stop their shaking. "I think I fell in love with her in that moment."

"I understand, Bobo," Jessie said. "When I stopped to change Dori's flat tire, it felt like I found something that was missing, the other half of my heart." He looked over at AJ who had turned to face him. "The first time I saw her, I was a goner. Every time she flinches when I touch her, it makes me want to punch someone. Someone treated her badly, and I really want to rearrange his face."

"Glad to know it's not just me. I think it's a Monroe thing, this falling in love at first sight," AJ said with a smile. "Remember Dad telling us how he fell in love with Mom the first time he saw her at that dance? After that first glance, there was no one else for him, not even after she died."

"Remember how Dad could always make her giggle like a schoolgirl? Her love for him shone in her eyes for the world to see." Jessie smiled. "I never believed him when he told us about that night they met, but now I do. I have this connection with Dori that I can't explain." He turned and reached into his pocket. "I bought this yesterday after I met her." He showed AJ the engagement ring. "I know she is the one. It's hard to believe I just met her yesterday."

AJ grinned. "Congrats, Jess! I guess it runs in the family," he said with a laugh. He opened his hand and showed Jessie the ring he bought for Rina after their kiss behind the barn, marveling at the similarity of the rings. "How did we both meet the girl for us in the same week? It's got to be a twin thing."

Rina looked up from the cutting board where she was slicing tomatoes for the sandwiches when AJ and Jessie walked into the kitchen. "Where did you two disappear to?" she asked as she continued slicing.

He took the knife out of her hand and laid it on the cutting board next to the tomato. "We were talking about the two girls we met recently and how they make us feel." He sat in one of the chairs around the kitchen table, pulling her down into his lap. "I was going to wait for the perfect time, but I can't think of a better time to do this than with my brother here."

He dug around in his pocket, almost panicking when he didn't feel the ring at first. He pulled the ring out, keeping it hidden from Rina. "I have a question I want to ask you. I know we've only known each other a little over a week, but I just can't wait any longer." He stood and sat Rina on the chair as he bent down onto one knee. "The first moment I saw you, my heart felt like it had come home. Will you marry me, Rina?" He watched her face, hoping he wouldn't see horror at his question.

Rina looked down at the ring in AJ's hand, hiding her shocked expression behind the hair hanging in her face. She looked up and smiled at the uncertainty in AJ's face. "Yes, I will."

AJ didn't move, willing his heart to start beating again as her words sunk in. "Yes?" He let out the breath he was holding in fear. At her nod, he stood and scooped her up into his arms. "Thank God," he whispered. He lowered his lips to hers and kissed her with everything in his heart.

Dori and Jessie turned and tiptoed out of the kitchen, letting them have some time alone.

Dori looked up at Jessie. "They just met this week? Wow, that's fast but so romantic." She turned and walked toward the bedrooms, hoping that Jessie didn't hear the wistfulness in her voice. "They'll probably be all lovey-dovey now," she muttered, trying to keep the envy and jealousy out of her voice. She jumped when she felt a hand drop onto her shoulder, relaxing when she realized it was Jessie.

"You're jealous!" he crowed, hoping against hope that he was right. "You girls all seem to love romantic gestures." He grinned as the ring seemed to burn a hole in his pocket. As much as he wanted to whip it out and ask her right now, he knew it wasn't the right time. "I've got an idea. Want to help?" He grabbed her hand and pulled her to the front door. "Let's go!"

Forty minutes later, they returned to Jessie's house.

Rina noticed the guitar case. "What's that for? Do you play?"

Jessie just grinned as he opened the case and pulled out the guitar.

AJ smiled. "That's where you disappeared to for so long. I wondered where you two were."

"I made a promise to Mom and Dad that if you ever got engaged, I would sing this song for you and your fiancée."

The strings vibrated with sound as he strummed the first chord. AJ's eyes shone with unshed tears, testament to how much he was moved by this simple act.

AJ pulled Rina to her feet and into his arms, holding her close and swaying to the music as Dori added her voice to Jessie's. By the end of the song, everyone was trying to hide the intense effect the song had on them.

AJ looked down at Rina. "I know it was quick, but I just couldn't wait. The Monroe men fall fast, and they fall forever."

They all sat around the table as Jessie and AJ reminisced about their parents and the love they shared. Rina and Dori both sighed, loving the story of love at first sight and marriage at nineteen that lasted until their last breath.

After a couple of hours, both AJ and Jessie realized that no one had been watching the shelter for most of the afternoon.

"We better get over there," AJ remarked as he helped clean up the dishes from lunch. "I hope nothing happened while we were here celebrating." He smiled looking over at Rina wiping off the table. "I am such a lucky guy."

Jessie put the last plate in the cupboard before he turned to AJ. "You ready to go? The girls can come over later. I'm sure they want to spend some time giggling over that ring."

At AJ's nod, Jessie walked over to Dori and let her know they were headed to Rina's.

She looked up into his eyes, seeming to like what she found there. "We'll be over later. We need to start discussing the wedding."

"Already? They haven't even set a date yet." Jessie grinned. "What is it with girls and weddings?"

Dori punched him in the arm. "That's enough out of you. Go take care of the dogs." She reached up and pulled him down to her for a quick kiss before she pushed him toward the door. "And take your brother with you!" she said as she spied AJ and Rina in a lip-lock.

Jessie grabbed AJ and pulled him away from Rina. "Come on, Romeo. We've got a job to do now. There will be time for that later." He pulled his brother out the door, laughing at his dazed expression. "You are such a goner."

"Just wait and see how you feel when Dori has your ring on her finger. The feeling is incredible." They strolled toward the barn, grinning like a couple of idiots.

Chapter Fourteen

RINA AND DORI poured a couple glasses of sweet tea and headed out on the deck, pulling two chairs over to the railing so they could look out over the fields in back of the house.

"So," Dori began, "how's it feel to be engaged? That was so romantic." She stared off into the distance, a faraway look in her eyes, dreaming of the day she would get her happily ever after. "How did you know he's the one?"

"I don't know. I just know that I would never be the same if he were no longer in my life. I can't believe I love him so much after just a few days." Rina looked down at the ring on her finger. "This all feels like a dream."

"Well, it's not a dream, so you need to start thinking about what kind of wedding you want. Large or small, indoor or outdoor ceremony, or you could just run off to Vegas and elope. If you go to Vegas, you better take me with you." She smiled at the thought of her friend marrying someone who seemed as great as AJ. That thought brought up images of Jessie and those eyes that seemed to be able to see down into her soul.

"Earth to Dori." Rina snickered. "Gee, I wonder where you went. You were thinking about Jessie, weren't you?"

Dori blushed. "How did you guess? I just want someone to love me like AJ loves you." Dori turned to Rina. "He seems to be a good guy, but I don't know if I can commit to a relationship again after all I went through with Ty."

Rina sipped her tea, trying to decide if she should ask Dori about Ty. It was obvious something bad had happened to send Dori running back to Woodview alone. "What happened with Ty?" Scooting her chair closer to Dori's, Rina questioned her further. "I can tell it was something bad. Please tell me. Maybe I can help."

"The only thing that would help would be if Ty fell off the face of the earth forever. He's an asshole, and I don't want anything to do with him."

Rina put her hand over Dori's. "Tell me what happened so I know how much to hate him. Seriously, you need to tell me." She brushed the hair out of Dori's eyes. "You know I won't judge."

Dori turned her face away from Rina, not wanting her to see her tears. "It started out as pinches when I did something he didn't like. After a while, it was slaps, and it gradually escalated to him using his belt on me.

Chapter Fifteen

TWO DAYS LATER, AJ and Jessie were driving back to the shelter after picking up dog food and other supplies in town. They noticed black smoke rising toward the sky off in the distance. AJ wondered who was burning trash on such a windy day. A sinking feeling in his stomach grew the closer they got to Rina's. The smoke was coming from somewhere near her place. They pulled into the driveway and discovered the black smoke was pouring from the back half of the barn.

Slamming on the brakes, AJ threw the SUV into park and jumped out. He ran toward the barn, Jessie at his heels telling the 911 operator they needed the fire department.

AJ threw open the door, yelling for Rina. The dogs barked as he searched for Rina, finding her in the storage room oblivious to the fire. "Rina, thank God! The barn is on fire. You've got to get out of here!"

"On fire?" The smoke rapidly started seeped into the

storage room. "The dogs!" She held her hand over her mouth, coughing and choking on the smoke. "We've got to get them out!" She ran toward the kennels.

Jessie grabbed her arm. "Get out, Rina! AJ and I will get the dogs."

"No! I'm not leaving them!"

"Get out, AJ. I'll come back for the dogs."

Afraid there wouldn't be time to get back in to save the dogs, he watched as Jessie led Rina toward the door before turning and running into the smoke-filled kennel area.

The smoke was getting thicker. AJ coughed as he used his hands to feel his way to the kennels. He opened the doors one by one and put the dogs on leashes. The dogs led him out of the barn where he found Jessie holding on to Rina to keep her from running back into the barn.

"Petey! Where's Petey?" She began to sob. "I shut him in the office when I went into the storeroom."

The smoke billowed out of every door and window.

AJ turned and ran back into the barn as they started hearing sirens.

Jessie squinted through the thick, black smoke, waving his hand in front of him in attempt to spot his brother. "AJ! The fire department is almost here. Wait for them! They have the equipment to deal with this!"

AJ ignored him. The thought of Rina losing Petey tore at his heart. He trotted into the barn and made his way to the office, coughing harder and harder every second. He heard Petey barking and clawing at the door. He opened the door and scooped Petey up into his arms, holding his shirt over Petey's face to try and filter some of the smoke.

He stumbled out of the barn, coughing and gasping for air. Rina twisted out of Jessie's grip and ran up to AJ and threw her arms around him. She pulled away and gently brushed the soot off his face. "Oh my God, AJ. Are you okay?"

AJ knelt to the ground and bent over trying to catch his breath. He let go of Petey who scurried over to Rina. "I'm okay," AJ said in between coughing fits. "Just need some fresh air."

Jessie frowned at AJ's wheezing. "Let me be the judge of that." He led AJ over to the ambulance that just drove up. "Cam, get the oxygen. AJ just had to play the hero." He made AJ sit on a gurney.

Cam handed him the oxygen mask. "You know the drill. Just sit here and breathe."

As soon as Jessie turned his back, Rina climbed up on the gurney next to AJ, pulled the oxygen mask down, and kissed him. She pulled away when he cut the kiss short to cough.

"Thank you for saving Petey," she said as she brushed the hair off his forehead. "Don't scare me like that again, okay?"

Jessie smiled at their kiss but frowned when AJ started coughing again. "Hey, enough of that for now," he said, checking the gauge on the oxygen tank after putting the oxygen mask back into place. "You need to go to the hospital, Bro. I don't like the sound of that wheezing." He closed his eyes and willed the memories back into the past, memories of asthma attacks and trips to the emergency room. Inhalers and breathing treatments were a part of life for AJ until they got it under control. "Hey, Cam, let's get the big hero to the hospital."

Cam had AJ lie down on the gurney, and he fastened the straps before they lifted it into the back of the ambulance.

Jessie took Petey from Rina and helped her step up into the ambulance for the ride to the hospital.

"Don't worry. I'll put the dogs in my back yard for now. We'll find something better for them tomorrow. I'll be at the hospital before you know it." He closed the ambulance doors and watched it drive off, concern for his brother evident on his face.

Rina held AJ's hand, trying to keep her worry from him. She talked about anything she could think of. "I was thinking that we should paint our bedroom a soft grey. And what do you think about a wood grain tile for the kitchen floor? You like deeper wood tones, right? A darker wood grain tile for our kitchen would look perfect."

AJ wheezed louder, struggling to breathe.

Rina looked at Cam with fear in her eyes.

She squeezed AJ's hand. "Come on, AJ. Breathe, honey. Stay with me."

"Love you, Rina," he whispered before he lost consciousness.

Cam tried to insert a breathing tube, but the swaying of the ambulance along with AJ's swollen airway made it almost impossible. With grim determination, he kept trying until he was finally successful. He attached the bag and squeezed it to breathe for AJ.

Rina watched in horror as Cam continued to compress the bag, essentially breathing for AJ. She squeezed AJ's hand, tears silently sliding down her cheeks.

"Don't you dare die on me now. You promised that everything would be okay. This is not okay." She put his hand up against her cheek and prayed, looking up only when the ambulance stopped and the doors opened.

"You have to let go now, Rina, so the doctors can help him," Cam explained as he jumped out of the ambulance still squeezing the bag. "Call Jessie!"

After getting all the dogs into his back yard, Jessie climbed into his truck still on the phone with the county SPCA making arrangements for them to find temporary homes for the dogs. He had just started the engine when he clapped his hand to his chest, gasping and struggling to breathe.

"God, no!" He zoomed out of the driveway, the gas pedal to the floor, not caring about anything but getting to AJ.

He answered his phone when it rang. "I'm on my way!"

Ten minutes later, he pulled up to the emergency room entrance and put his truck in neutral and pulled on the emergency brake, not bothering to shut it off or shut the door. He ran full out past the reception desk, ignoring the pain in his knee and the tightness in his chest as he heard a code blue to treatment room three. He halted when he saw the look on Rina's face, the worry and despair there for everyone to see. He grabbed her hand, and they waited. Time stood still until the doctor walked out of the treatment room with a grim look on his face. Rina dropped to the floor sobbing as Jessie kneeled next to her and held her closely. Their lives were now changed forever…

Chapter Sixteen

RINA WIPED AWAY a tear as she opened the door to the vestibule, taking Cam's arm after adjusting her dress.

"Hey, don't cry. You'll ruin your makeup."

"I don't know if I can do this, Cam. What if I get up there and I can't remember what I was going to say?"

He was prepared and pulled a couple of tissues out of his pocket. "See, there's Jessie. He's got a copy, and he'll help you get through it."

The organist played the first few notes of the song she had chosen, signaling the start of the service.

She looked toward the front of the church, gaining courage from the smile she saw on Jessie's face. He whispered to the man standing next to him with his back to her, bringing his attention to Rina.

The smile on AJ's face when he turned and saw Rina in her wedding dress lit up the whole church, making Rina smile in return and banishing the jitters she was feeling. A single tear escaped as she thought about how she once feared this day would never come.

AJ had been put in a medically induced coma and had to be on a ventilator for two weeks to let his lungs heal; to Rina, it had felt more like two months. The waiting and the worry were finally relieved when the day came that she could look into his eyes once again.

Struggling to keep his gaze on her tear-filled eyes, he whispered, "Love you, Rina." She smiled and hugged him, laying her head on his chest, listening to him breathe as she wept.

After the fire, the sheriff finally took her situation seriously and started investigating the incidents as crimes. A month later, Sid Nelson, the town drunk, was arrested when he tried to sabotage the rebuilding of the shelter by planting evidence of drug trafficking in Rina's house. Jessie caught him in the act, breaking Sid's nose and jaw before the police got there. Sid confessed to starting the fire. He had been paid by Mayor McMillan to get Rina to leave by whatever means necessary.

The mayor had tried for years to get Rina's grandfather to sell his land to him, claiming he wanted to raise horses. Shortly after he was arrested, an old letter from McMillan's father to Rina's great-grandfather was discovered, detailing how the mayor's father had lost the land to Rina's great-grandfather in a poker game. Over the years, the hatred between the two families grew until the mayor decided it was time to get the land back. Already harassing her through his protection racket, he upped the ante and paid Sid to step up the harassment.

Various charges were brought, from arson to animal cruelty. Rina's accounts were released, and a brand new state-of-the-art shelter was built with enough space to house fifty dogs.

The wedding progressed smoothly, other than Petey barking when AJ and Rina kissed for the first time as man and wife. Everyone laughed as Jessie picked up Petey to quiet him down. Gunner, always the perfect gentleman, sat next to Dori throughout the entire ceremony as if protecting her. After the wedding, everyone drove out to Rina's for the reception.

The leaves had turned and were falling from the trees, crunching underfoot as the guests walked to the large tent out in Rina's yard erected for the reception.

The reception was in full swing, the guests laughing and drinking and dancing. AJ and Rina danced to a song only they could hear. She settled against him, her ear to his chest listening to the steady thump of his heart.

"Love you, AJ."

"Love you more."

Dori watched her friend dancing with her new husband, wondering if she would ever feel safe enough to let Jessie know how she felt about him. Turning from the dance floor, she stumbled from a combination of alcohol and her heels. Jessie caught her and kept her from falling to the floor.

"I need to go get my flip flops before I break an ankle. I left them up in Rina's room in the house." She kissed him and stumbled toward the house, humming and thinking about Jessie's arms wrapped around her when they danced to the slow songs. She hurried up the stairs after slipping out of her shoes. She grabbed her flip flops out of the bag and put them on before stopping to check her reflection in the mirror. Her eyes sparkled, and her face was flushed from dancing; she looked happy. She ran down the stairs, yearning for the feel of Jessie's arms around her again.

She froze when a voice from her past whispered in her ear. "I finally have you alone. Your soldier boy can't save you now."

Before she could scream, a hand covered her mouth, mashing her lips against her teeth. Her assailant wrapped his other arm around her and pinned her to his side.

"You left. I didn't give you permission to leave. You'll pay for that," he growled as he dragged her down the porch steps toward his van.

About the Author

L.A. Remenicky writes love stories with a twist. A forty-something wife and mother of three fur kids, she works as a payroll professional by day and writes out the stories in her head by night.

An avid reader all her life, she finally put pen to paper (or fingers to keyboard) during NaNoWriMo in 2012 and has never looked back. When she's not typing away on her latest tale with music playing in the background, she can usually be found spending time with her family and friends.

You can follow L.A. at these locations:

Facebook: http://www.facebook.com/laremenicky
Twitter: http://www.twitter.com/remenickywrites
Newsletter signup: http://eepurl.com/O0b4H

Other works by L.A. Remenicky

http://amazon.com/author/laremenicky

Saving Cassie (Fairfield Corners Book 1) - Everyone has secrets. Sometimes secrets can get you killed. After ten years in the big city, Cassie Holt is moving back to her hometown to take over the bookstore left to her by her beloved Gram, vowing to live her life alone. To her best friend, Sheriff James Marsten, Cassie seems to be the same girl that left Fairfield Corners to go to college but Cassie has secrets and one of those secrets could get her killed. When one of her secrets becomes a threat to her life, James turns to his new deputy to help him keep Cassie safe. Deputy Logan Miller has been burned by love and is not looking to get involved with anyone anytime soon. When he is thrown into close quarters with Cassie, the sparks begin to fly and he begins to see through the walls Cassie has built around her heart. As the threat gets closer, can Logan protect Cassie and protect his heart? (Mature Adult, 18+)

Ragan's Song (Fairfield Corners Book 2) – It only took one look into his eyes for her to know she was in trouble. Adam Bricklin has heard the melody in his head for years, the melody that told him if a decision was right or wrong. When he met Ragan Newlin the song told him she was the one. He was devastated when circumstances tore them apart. It has taken three years for Adam to finally move past the heartbreak he suffered when Ragan left town in the middle of the night. No note, no email, no text. She was just gone. Now he has a new girlfriend, a new album in the works, and his daughter is doing well in school. Until the day Ragan returned to Fairfield Corners. Ragan came home to celebrate her parents' anniversary, hoping they would forgive her for not telling them about her marriage or her son. When she discovered that Adam was still living in Fairfield Corners she hoped her secrets were safe; secrets that drove her away three years ago, secrets that could change their lives forever.

Invisible - They found each other. Then the killer found them. Detective Jackson "Jax" McKenna walks into a psychologist's office and finds that the doctor bears a striking resemblance to his first love, Lainie, who disappeared ten years ago after their disastrous first date ended in violence. Dr. Elizabeth Parker is really Elaine Wilson. She's been in hiding since the night that changed both their lives. Can Jax save Lainie and help her stay Invisible? (Mature, 18+)

Where There's Faith (Fairfield Corners Book 3) - A past she can't remember. A love he can't forget. After losing everything in an accident that he can only blame himself for, Robbie Newlin embraced sobriety and tried to live his life quietly alone at this family's cottage on the lake. Grief being his only ally, Robbie was perfectly content with how he lived until Faith moved into the cottage next door. Now Faith had him questioning whether to keep grieving or to open his broken heart to let love in again. Faith McMillan had no memory of her life before that day three years ago. The physical scars had faded but the emotional ones were still fresh and raw. Living rent-free seemed like a great way to finish her second book and give her the time to figure out her next move, but then she met the reclusive guy next door and everything changed. To get past the broken parts, Robbie and Faith must figure out if they want to continue living their lives in solitude or take a chance on finding an ending together.

Loving Marie (A Fairfield Corners Prequel) - Falling in love with his partner's little sister was never part of the plan. There was an order to James Marsden's future: get a job as an Indianapolis cop, work his way up to detective, and then find a nice girl and start a family. He never planned on walking into a diner his first day as a rookie copy and for her to blow his entire timeline to smithereens. When Marie Griffen's older brother Steve introduced her to his new trainee, she was instantly drawn to his shy demeanor and blushing face. Only, she couldn't act on her feelings even if she wanted to. Steve wanted her to date someone with a normal job – that wasn't his partner. Marie just wanted to live her own life without her older brother watching over her. Marie and James must decide if this off-limits romance is worth the risk or if the consequences are too much for either of them to bear.

Last Chance Christmas (A Fairfields Novella) - From the outside, Brent Halston and Jordan McKenna had the perfect life: the house, the dog, fulfilling careers, and their love. However, Jordan's past refused to leave her alone, threatening to destroy all they had built together. Without explanation, Jordan pushed Brent out of her life, leaving him devastated and confused. In an attempt to start over, Brent relocated to Fairfield Corners, bought an extravagant house, and mourned the loss of his Jojo. To keep herself from drowning in her own grief, Jordan gave everything she had to her career as a doctor, running the free clinic on the rough side of town. As the holiday season approached, a frantic phone call from Jordan's brother pulled Brent back into Jordan's life, giving them the opportunity to reconnect. Battling the past and present, their love must survive secrets and betrayal, giving them one last chance to be together.

Loving Jessie's Girl (Love On The Double – Book 1) - Until AJ Monroe left Indiana after college he had always lived in his identical twin brother's shadow. He had made a life for himself in Denver, Colorado, away from Jessie, away from Indiana. But when AJ feared for his brother's safety, he left everything behind to step back into the shadow he thought he had outgrown. Finding his brother was AJ's only concern...until he met Jessie's girl. Fiercely independent, Rina Abbot hid her true situation from everyone, including her best friend, Jessie. Out of money and unable to care for her rescue dogs she had no choice but to accept the help of the handsome stranger with a familiar face. Afraid to trust him, she tried to ignore the feelings he stirred within her as they searched for his missing brother. But secrets never stay secrets for long. Finally open about their feelings for each other, Rina's secrets began to wreak havoc on their lives. Would Rina's secrets force AJ to give up his dream of loving Jessie's girl?

Also from the Lavish Publishing Family

Summer Spirit Series

Samantha Jacobey

http://myBook.to/SummerSpiritSeries

No one EVER had a summer romance like this!

When Charlie visited another plane parallel to our own, he discovered that Summer Angels and Dark Angels battle over the fate of man.

Faced with choices no one should ever have to make, his adventure has been fraught with twists and turns, with life and death hanging in the balance. His guardian, Clarisse, is the half that makes him whole, but sinister forces conspire to do more than simply keep them apart.

Find out if they can stand up to the powers that be in this THRILLING MAGICAL ADVENTURE!!!

The Norn Novellas

A. Nicky Hjort

http://myBook.to/NornNovellas

The Norn Novellas are all chapters in the epic saga of the youngest and most fickle of the four Norn Sisters. The same feisty immortal creature who must escape her inherent inner darkness to learn the meaning of life.

Each story takes a classic fairytale and spins it on its head, as we learn that maybe Norse Mythology was so much more than legend. And to think, you thought you knew those old tales so well.

Meet Za and find out what really happened...

www.ingramcontent.com/pod-product-compliance
Lightning Source LLC
Chambersburg PA
CBHW060353180626
46817CB00008B/2995